Radar looked to the pair and then back, tilting his head. Gabe clucked his tongue. "What makes you think I'm even interested?"

Wagging his tail and panting, Radar pressed against Gabe's leg.

"Okay, sure, she's cute and I didn't see a wedding ring." Yeah, okay, he might've checked. He noisily blew out air between his lips. Why did he do that?

"But even if she's single, she can't be more than early twenties. That's too young." *Are you sure?* his inner voice taunted. Because the way that heart-shaped butt filled out those jeans and those hips swayed as Addie walked away didn't look too young.

Radar started forward as the pair put more distance between them, and Gabe tightened his grip on the leash. Glancing up, Radar tried out his forlorn *life is so unfair* whine. How was a guy supposed to hold out against that oh-so-expressive head tilt and impressive vocal range?

* * *

SMALL-TOWN SWEETHEARTS:
Small towns, huge passi

Dear Reader,

As an animal lover, I enjoy including them in my stories, but that old Hollywood adage about not working with kids or animals because they steal the scene also applies to writing!

As soon as he appeared on the page, Radar became a character in his own right and all the prewriting plans I had for him went out the window. He had his own agenda, but luckily, it aligned with mine for Gabe and Addie.

Thank goodness my local veterinarian is not just my cats' doctor but also a fan of my stories. Once she got over her initial dismay at what I was asking, she was helpful and wrote down all sorts of information. Please note that no dogs were injured during the writing of this story.

I love to hear from my readers. You may email me at authorcarrienichols@gmail.com. I'd love to hear about your furbabies.

Carrie

The Sergeant's Matchmaking Dog

CARRIE NICHOLS

HARLEQUIN
SPECIAL
EDITION

Recycling programs for this product may not exist in your area.

ISBN-13: 978-1-335-40796-2

The Sergeant's Matchmaking Dog

Copyright © 2021 by Carol Opalinski

For questions and comments about the quality of this book, please contact us at CustomerService@Harlequin.com.

Harlequin Enterprises ULC
22 Adelaide St. West, 40th Floor
Toronto, Ontario M5H 4E3, Canada
www.Harlequin.com

Printed in U.S.A.

Carrie Nichols grew up in New England but moved south and traded snow for central AC. She loves to travel, is addicted to British crime dramas and knows a *Seinfeld* quote appropriate for every occasion.

A 2016 RWA Golden Heart® Award winner and two-time Maggie Award for Excellence winner, she has one tolerant husband, two grown sons and two critical cats. To her dismay, Carrie's characters—like her family—often ignore the wisdom and guidance she offers.

Books by Carrie Nichols

Harlequin Special Edition

Small-Town Sweethearts

The Marine's Secret Daughter
The Sergeant's Unexpected Family
His Unexpected Twins
The Scrooge of Loon Lake
The Sergeant's Matchmaking Dog

Visit the Author Profile page
at Harlequin.com for more titles.

This book is dedicated to the wonderful vets
and staff at Banfield Pet Hospital Hixson.
They have not only taken wonderful care of my
beloved furbabies but helped with my fictional one.

Chapter One

"C'mon, what's wrong with that one? Looks like a perfectly good bush to me." Former marine staff sergeant Gabe Bishop sighed as he glanced at what seemed like an endless row of forsythia bushes. Their bright yellow blooms created a natural fence between the still-dormant grass of someone's lawn and the cracked concrete of the sidewalk where he stood.

"Just pick one…any one…" He rubbed a hand over the scratchy stubble peppering his chin. "Please."

Suspending his search for the perfect spot to relieve himself, Radar lifted his head to give Gabe a long-suffering look. As if his human companion should understand the protocols by now.

"I should be training you—" Gabe yawned "—not the other way around."

He still had to lug in all those storage boxes crowded in the back of his Jeep Sahara. But what he longed for most was a hot shower after being on the road for close to twenty hours, fueled by truck-stop coffee and a quick nap at a rest area.

The animal went back to examining the bushes and Gabe sighed again. "You can bet marine dogs perform on command."

Radar whined his displeasure and Gabe regretted the disparaging remark. The dog might bear an un-canny resemblance to the Belgian Malinois the mili-tary favored, but Radar had been only the camp mutt, a mascot of sorts. Despite the circumstances, Gabe considered Radar's contribution to their squad every bit as valuable as sniffing for explosives. Radar's mere presence had boosted the morale of those men and women stationed so far from home, family and everything familiar.

Gabe might have told himself he'd been honoring a promise while he fought bureaucratic red tape to get the dog stateside, but that was simply an excuse.

The truth was he hated to think of what Radar's fate might have been if he'd been abandoned after command had ordered the evacuation of their forlorn desert outpost. Yeah, like he wouldn't have done his damnedest—promise or no—to get Radar to safety.

Radar had never been an active marine, and since

his honorable discharge last Friday, neither was he. Even if he was no longer addressed as SSgt. Bishop in daily life, that identity would always be a part of him. A rank he was proud to have attained. Once a marine, always a marine. *Oo-rah!*

The irony didn't escape him that civilian Gabe was a lot like Radar—searching for a perfect bush. Huh. "Sorry, buddy. I—"

A drilling clatter had him tensing and scanning his surroundings for anomalies. Same blue-collar neighborhood lined mostly with single-family brick ranches and a few duplexes like his rental unit. Nothing had changed from five minutes ago. So, what—?

The noise sounded again. Spotting a red-bellied woodpecker drumming an aluminum rain gutter, Gabe relaxed his guard and snorted a laugh. Looked like Radar wasn't the only one intent on marking his territory this sunny April afternoon.

He shook his head. Such vigilance. What had he been expecting? This was Loon Lake, a place that travel brochures had dubbed quintessential New England. It boasted of a grass-covered town square and the ubiquitous eighteenth-century white clapboard church with a soaring steeple. Brick-fronted small businesses with colorful awnings and antique-looking streetlights crowded along Main Street. Despite appearances, the awnings and white-globed lamps were new.

Gabe grinned. How much squabbling had taken

place before the town council voted to approve those lamps? He may have been barely twenty when he'd left for basic, but he knew residents enjoyed nothing better than arguing over mundane details. Pa had come home from those meetings grumbling about—

Radar pulled on the lead, jerking Gabe out of his thoughts and back to practical matters, like getting back to the rented duplex to finish unpacking so he could settle in and begin his new life. Whatever that might look like. With his pa gone, he had no relatives in Loon Lake, but the town was still home.

He tried to turn them around, but Radar dropped down on his belly in the middle of the sidewalk. Gabe tugged again on the leash, but the dog wouldn't budge.

"What have I told you about mission creep?" he asked, referring to a shift in objectives that resulted in further commitment and time. The dog whined and Gabe shook his head. "Fine, a couple more blocks, but that's it. I can haul your seventy-five-pound butt home if I have to. Don't think I won't."

Radar rose and did a full-body shake, his tags jingling merrily. Gabe narrowed his eyes at the dog's actions—looked like this human needed to practice his alpha-dog skills. They continued to the end of the street and turned to follow the sidewalk along a wider, busier road.

Sure, they didn't have to worry about snipers or improvised explosive devices, but being so exposed made his scalp prickle. He disliked that feeling of being watched, even benignly, and he'd already pegged the woman across the street as a curtain twitcher.

At least no one had shown up on his doorstep with casseroles or baked goods—yet. And with any luck, they wouldn't. He'd had enough handouts in his childhood to last a lifetime.

"Yeah, I know what you're thinking, dog. Why come home if I wanted to avoid attention?" Truth was he'd been yearning for something familiar, and his memories of growing up in Loon Lake weren't all bad. And frankly, after being away for a decade, he assumed the residents' memories of the kid with the free lunches and hand-me-down clothes would have dimmed. Even if the legacy of the teen who'd learned to cover embarrassment by acting tough and getting into trouble hadn't been erased.

After Radar had marked a tree, a lamppost and an azalea bush—apparently those were acceptable— Gabe succeeded in coaxing him to head toward home. As they approached their street, a school bus stopped with a squeal of the air brakes and a hiss as the pneumatic door swung open. Hoping to get away before any kids got off, he pulled on the leash, but Radar sat on his haunches, once again refusing to move. Damn, but he was going to have to establish who was in charge in this relationship.

The dog stared intently at the bus, his ears thrust

forward. When he whined, Gabe gave him a pat on the head. "I guess this is your first time seeing one of those, huh?"

A bespectacled boy wearing a gray T-shirt, jeans and black Chuck Taylor high-tops bounded off the steps. The kid's mouth formed a giant O and he made a beeline toward them, his backpack bouncing around his thin shoulders. Gabe zeroed in on that backpack and tensed, but Radar whimpered and pressed against him, grounding him, bringing him back to the moment and their surroundings.

"What a cool dog, mister." The boy, who appeared to be around six or seven, dropped to his knees and thrust out a hand to pet Radar on the head. "Is it a he or a she? What's his name? Is he yours? What kind is it?"

As Gabe was trying to decide which question to answer first, running footsteps pounded on the pavement behind them. Reacting to the threat, he spun around. A woman sprinted toward them, a blond ponytail tied high on her head bouncing along behind her. He assumed a protective crouch and unconsciously reached for his hip—for the weapon that had been his constant companion for the past decade.

Radar whined and once again broke the spell. Although the dog hadn't acted in any official capacity, he'd alerted them to enemy advances on the compound, saving them from surprise attacks. But no hostiles or suicide bombers looking to kill them here. Trying to get his heart out of his throat, he swallowed and straightened up.

"Theodore Andrew Miller, what do you think you're doing?" The woman skidded to a stop, her pink-and-purple sneakers scattering pebbles. She gulped in air. "What have I told you about approaching strange animals?"

"But it's not a strange animal. It's a dog." The boy scrunched up his face, and the tops of his brown-framed eyeglasses shot past his eyebrows. "See?"

Gabe coughed to disguise the laugh that had bubbled up, and the woman threw an angry scowl in his direction. She had pale blue eyes, a small turned-up nose and freckles sprinkled high across her cheeks. And, oh yeah, she was spitting mad. And kind of young to be this kid's mother. But who was he to judge? Especially considering his past.

"Teddy, I saw you rushing up to him with your hand out," she said. "That dog could've bitten your fingers off."

Her scolding may have been directed at the boy, but Gabe bristled as if those words had been tossed his way. People could think what they wanted about him, but he wasn't about to allow anyone to label Radar a menace. "Ma'am, my dog wouldn't hurt anybody."

She dismissed his words with a wave of her hand. "How was Teddy supposed to know that?"

Okay, so she had a point. He scratched the scruff

on his cheek, debating how best to proceed. "If it helps, I'm not a complete stranger to—"

"You're a stranger to us," she said, critically eyeing him up and down as if he and his dog didn't belong on this well-tended street.

"Excuse me, ma'am, but my dog is leashed as required by law. *Your* boy approached us, not the other way around. So, if anyone's to blame, it's him." Heat crept up his neck and settled in his cheeks. Could he get any lower, shifting fault to a kid? Even if it was the truth.

The boy held up a hand, turning it over several times, and Gabe winced at the burn scars on both sides.

"See," he said. "The dog didn't bite me."

"This time," the woman said.

"Will your dog be happy to see me from now on, just like today, mister?" The boy plunged his fingers into the thick fur on Radar's neck.

Gabe nodded, but there wouldn't be a "from now on" if he could help it. He planned on a hassle-free civilian life. His immediate future would consist of finding a job and maybe catching up with a few friends from school.

"See? It's okay because the doggy's going to be nice to me the next time too," the boy said, sounding like that settled the matter. Radar drummed his tail on the sidewalk, and the kid gave him a hug.

The woman closed her eyes, and her lips moved

as if she were counting or praying for patience at the child's literal directness. Gabe cleared his throat, and her eyes flew open.

"Teddy, you know better than to talk to strangers. Especially ones with—" she threw another mistrustful glance at Radar "—dogs."

Gabe tightened his fingers around the leash. Okay, now he was pissed. He may have found her appealing in a fresh-faced, wholesome sort of way, but her attitude was sticking in his craw. "Look, lady, I don't know what you have against dogs, but—"

"I have nothing against dogs," she rushed to supply. "But, as I've explained to Teddy, some predators use them to lure unsuspecting children. It, uh, it was nothing personal," she said, a slight blush spreading across her cheeks, highlighting all those tiny freckles. "I apologize if it came across as an insult."

He clamped his mouth shut on the stinging retort that had sprung to his lips. Huh. Her reasoning made sense. How could he argue against child safety? He wouldn't, because he was leaving, getting away from her, her strangely alluring freckles and her kid. He'd go home and take that shower and clean up as he'd planned before Radar had hijacked the mission.

Aside from moving and opening the rest of those storage boxes, the most drama scheduled for today was plopping on the couch and watching some spring baseball, maybe sipping a cold brew. Whether that cold brew would be coffee or beer had yet to be determined. His gaze roamed over the woman and those blue eyes shooting fire at him.

Beer was in the lead.

"You weren't even at the stop when the bus came," the kid said, as if sensing a weakness he could exploit.

"You're right—that's my fault. That last batch of cupcakes took longer to bake than I anticipated." She grimaced. "And, of course, this is the first time in a month that damn bus has been on time."

Gasping, the boy unfolded and sprang up like a marionette whose strings had been pulled taut. "Uh-oh, you have to put a quarter in the jar for using that word. You made me last week, so it's only fair that you do too."

"I have a feeling I owe more than a quarter after nearly suffering a heart attack. C'mon, Teddy, we need to get home." She held out her hand, her gaze darting between the boy and Radar.

The kid scowled. "But I didn't even get to find out the dog's name or nothin'."

"His name's Radar," Gabe told him. Maybe that would pacify the child and he'd allow her to lead him away.

"There. You know his name. Let's go." She had a death grip on the boy's hand and began marching away but threw a cautious glance over her shoulder.

Teddy twisted around and raised his free hand. "Bye, Radar. Bye, mister."

"What happened to the jacket you had on this morning?" the woman asked as they walked away.

"I dunno… Musta left it at school." The response drifted back to them, and Radar gave a low woof, then whined.

"Listen to you." Gabe rubbed the soft fur behind the dog's ears. "You'd think you were losing your best friend in the world."

The woman was saying something, but they were too far away to make out the words, and Radar whined again.

"Forget it, dog," Gabe muttered. "We don't need any part of whatever they've got going on. From now on, we're in a no-drama zone."

Radar looked to the pair and then back, tilting his head. Gabe clucked his tongue. "What makes you think I'm even interested?"

Wagging his tail and panting, Radar pressed against Gabe's leg.

"Okay, sure, she's cute and I didn't see a wedding ring." Yeah, okay, he might've checked. He noisily blew out air between his lips. Why did he do something as silly as scan for a sign that she was off-limits? He wasn't even looking for any sort of relationship.

Radar made a nonmenacing growling noise deep in his throat.

"Look, even if she's single, she can't be more than early twenties. That's too young." *Are you sure?* his inner voice taunted. Because the way that heart-shaped butt filled out those jeans and those hips swayed as she walked away didn't look too young.

Radar started forward as the pair put more distance between them, and Gabe tightened his grip on the leash. Glancing up, Radar tried out his forlorn life-is-so-unfair whimper. How was a guy supposed to hold out against that oh-so-expressive head tilt and impressive vocal range?

"Forget it. I'm not in the market. Even if I was—which I'm not—my thirty going on fifty is definitely too old for all that fresh-faced innocence." He snorted. Was this what his life had come to? From maintaining the discipline and efficiency of the men under his command with field training exercises to arguing with a dog over a woman?

Radar auditioned a different sound, but Gabe stood firm. "What do you know? You're a dog. My guess is she had your undying devotion when she mentioned she baked cupcakes."

He patted Radar on the head and exhaled. "Temptation, thy name is woman."

Radar looked up at him and Gabe shook his head. "Yeah, I have no idea where that came from either."

But he did know the blonde walking away was temptation, and in his experience, that path generally ended with trouble.

Thankfully, those scrapes were nothing more than teenage antics, like the time he'd tried to hijack a rival school's stuffed mascot. Those shenanigans could be traced back to his desire to impress a certain cheerleader. Tracy Harris. Yeah, he'd impressed himself right into a shotgun wedding upon graduation.

He knew better now, and this woman, with that sweet face, had to be the kind of woman who was all in…marriage, kids and forever. So he was going to avoid her—and temptation. Getting the rest of his life on a good track was his first—and last—priority.

He had enough old mistakes on his conscience. He didn't want any new ones.

Been there. Done that.

Even though Teddy was unharmed, Addie Miller's heart continued its staccato rhythm as they headed toward home. Seeing her brother running up to that humongous dog and being too far away to do anything had scared the holy— Oops! She owed the swear jar enough quarters for one day. Nothing like feeling helpless to bring out her potty mouth. She may have needed that tough exterior as protection in the past, but now that she was responsible for Teddy, she needed to set a good example.

Inappropriate language aside, she'd had to acknowledge the sickening truth. If something had happened to Teddy today, the blame would've been hers and hers alone. How could she have allowed baking cupcakes—or anything at all—to distract her?

Queasiness roiled her stomach. Were her promises meaningless too? Was this how she made up for not being there for Teddy in the past?

If he'd gotten mauled by a dog or snatched by a stranger, that would make her no better than their mother, Michelle. And she'd owe an apology to those social workers who'd warned her she'd been ill-equipped to take on such an enormous responsibility, caring for her much younger half brother at her age. She couldn't magically change how many years she'd been on this earth, but she could step up and do what was necessary.

She glanced at Teddy's hand in hers and, seeing the burn scars marring his hand and wrist, choked back a sob. Although she'd been away at college when he'd plunged his hands into scalding hot water, she blamed herself for not being there to prevent it. The fact her brother's care had been her mother's responsibility, and not hers, never mattered one whit to Addie's conscience.

"Addie?" Teddy squeezed her hand and frowned. "It's okay. Radar didn't hurt me. He was a really, really nice doggy," he added in a wistful tone.

Addie blinked against the burn in her eyes. "I'm sure he was, but—"

"—dogs are expensive," he finished for her and kicked a pebble across the sidewalk until it disappeared into a thicket of forsythia bushes. "Joey Johnson said people give puppies away for free when they don't want them. Maybe we could get one like that."

"Even if we did, veterinary care costs lots of money." Her conscience was a hot poker, jabbing her for using the trite excuse. "It wasn't just about the dog, sweetie. That man you spoke to was a stranger. Do you remember how I've asked you not to talk to strangers?"

Teddy's chin hiked up. "You talked to him."

"Yes, I did, but I'm an adult and—"

He pulled his hand from her grip, crossed his arms over his chest and stuck them under his armpits. "But you're my sister. How come you get to act all adult? Make rules for me and stuff like that? Joey's older sister doesn't do that."

Because you deserve a responsible adult in your life. Tag, she was it. "I was lucky enough to be born first, and you know how much I like having you live with me. You know that, don't you?"

He nodded but stuck out his lower lip. "But it's still not fair."

Life rarely is. She ruffled his hair, a gesture Teddy said was for babies, but even as he ducked to get away, she saw his lips twitch as he fought a smile.

"If you like having me live with you so much, why won't you let me walk home from the bus stop alone?" His expression turned calculating. "I'm big enough, and besides, all the kids on the bus laugh because they know you're my sister."

Her stomach flip-flopped. She understood that he might find her presence embarrassing. How many times had Michelle embarrassed her by showing up at school functions high, inappropriately dressed or hanging off the arm of some guy who was most likely her dealer? Oh, how she'd longed for a mom who volunteered to bake cupcakes for school parties or chaperoned field trips.

She sighed. Was it too much to ask that Teddy wait until after the hearing for permanent custody to go through a rebellious phase? She didn't trust their mother to keep her word about not fighting it. The family counselor she'd spoken with had assured her that Teddy's actions were a good thing. Testing boundaries meant he felt safe living with her. "I understand how you feel, sweetie, but maybe we—"

"Hey, look! Radar is following us."

She whipped around, and sure enough, the man and his dog had closed the distance between them. This time she concentrated on the owner. He was at least two, maybe three, inches over six feet, with thick brown hair that spiked on top but was cut shorter on the sides. He had straight dark eyebrows above a hawk nose and generous lips surrounded by a thick sprinkling of dark stubble. How had she not noticed he had the most amazing hazel eyes? Or that despite the dusty and torn clothing, he didn't look as disreputable as she'd first assumed. How had she not noticed any of those details before now?

Maybe because the dog had scared the crap out of you. Still does.

She turned back to her brother. "Teddy, why don't you run on ahead? I frosted a cupcake for you and set it aside. And you can play some *Mario Kart.*"

"Why?" Teddy's eyes narrowed behind his glasses. "What's going on that you don't want me to know about?"

"Nothing is going on." She pressed a hand to her stomach. To think she'd been thankful when Teddy had started coming out of his shell, had started feeling comfortable enough to question her. "You're the one always begging me for more video-game time."

"But I want to see where Radar is going."

So did she. She'd resided here long enough to know everyone on the street at least well enough to wave when they drove by.

And she'd definitely remember both of them.

Chapter Two

Man and dog caught up to them before she could order Teddy inside. The animal sat at the man's feet when he stopped. Obedient, but excited shivers coursed through its body.

Was it possible for a dog to yearn? If so, this one did it every time he glanced at Teddy. Her heart constricted. She was still fearful, but maybe it was time—past time—to face this fear straight on and put it behind her.

If only… She reached out blindly for Teddy's hand because fears weren't wished away.

"Are you lost, or did you need something?" she asked, trying to sound polite, but it came out as more of an accusation than an inquiry.

The man held his hands up, palms out, the leash threaded through the fingers of one hand. "Neither one. We're just minding our own business and going home."

He had large, calloused hands with blunt-tipped—Wait... What? "Home?"

He nodded and pointed. "This is us, the duplex up there on the left."

He was indicating the house with brick on the bottom, blue clapboards on the upper half and black shutters. One of only two multifamily dwellings on the street, it was well cared for, and like the other homes, it was set back to allow for a decent-sized front yard. Despite being only a renter, she felt a sense of pride being able to offer her brother such a stable—

"Oh boy! Did you hear that?" Teddy tugged on her hand, bringing her back to the current situation. "Radar's moving in with us."

Teddy did a little dance and the dog's plumy tail waved in an arc as if he too was celebrating this happy news. The dog who was invading her space.

Clearing his throat, the stranger rubbed a hand across his mouth and met her gaze. Those mesmerizing eyes seemed to both mock and challenge her. As if he had read her mind.

"Did you know only 5 percent of the population have hazel eyes?" she asked.

"What?" He blinked and frowned, furrowing the skin between his brows.

Her face flamed. Damn her encyclopedic brain that collected trivia. Her thirst for knowledge came in handy at her job as a library assistant, but not so much when the information she retained spewed back up at the most inopportune times. "Nothing. I—"

"She was talking about eye color and—"

"Teddy, why don't you go inside…? Now."

"But—but—"

"You may as well listen to her." He pinned her with his gaze. "Radar and I are heading to the previously *unoccupied* side, if that makes you feel any better."

No, it didn't make her feel any better because that enormous dog would be living… Right. Next. Door.

Teddy scrunched his nose. "What does un— unoccupied mean?"

"Empty," she answered automatically, her mind still processing the fact they were her new neighbors. She shook her head. "But—but I spoke with Natalie a few days ago and she didn't tell me anyone was moving in."

He lifted a broad shoulder in a negligible shrug. "You'll have to take that up with the person who actually owns the house."

"Sam's mom owns the house," Teddy said, the man's sarcasm going over his head. "Are you and

Radar new in town? We used to be new, didn't we, Addie?"

"Actually, I grew up in Loon Lake, but I've been away for over ten years," the man said.

"Wow, that's a long time." Teddy's eyes widened. "Were you in jail, like—?"

"Teddy! You're being rude." She squeezed his shoulder but felt like a hypocrite because he was asking the questions she was too polite to voice. Exactly who was this new neighbor and where had he been for ten years? Her curiosity was justified because she had social workers combing through her life, checking Teddy's living arrangements. Really? Like that justified being nosy or judgmental about a stranger?

And underneath all that justification was the fact that Teddy's life experiences—like her own—had him making the leap from *absence* to *jail*.

Teddy hung his head. "Sorry for being rude."

"I'm sure your mother will be relieved to know I wasn't incarcerated. I—"

"Addie's not my mother." Teddy's head popped up. "Even if she acts like it and I live with her. She's just my sister."

She winced at his use of the qualifier *just*. Despite what anyone said, she didn't need him testing her authority. Not now. Could he say something like that to a social worker or judge?

"Then your sister will be happy to know I've been in the marines, not jail." He quirked an eyebrow at her as if to say he'd known she'd been as curious as her brother.

Teddy's eyes lit up. "The marines! Was Radar with you too?"

She tried to disguise her relief and… "The marines? That means you must be Gabriel Bishop, the war hero everyone has been—"

Oh God, Addie, just shut up. Running your mouth isn't helping.

"I see gossip is still the number one sport in Loon Lake," he said with a cynical twist of his lips.

Before Addie could form a response, Teddy rambled on. "Is Radar a war hero too? Did he wear all the cool stuff like I seen in that movie about the military dog? Remember that movie we saw, Addie?" Teddy leaned closer to the dog, trying to drag her with him. "The one in the movie had a vest and goggles just like the soldiers, but they were all dog-sized. Does Radar have all that 'quipment?"

"No. He didn't have any of that. He was—" The dog woofed and tilted his head to look up at his owner, who reached down and scratched him behind the ears. "But he was every bit a member of our squad. He was one of us."

That canine mouth pulled back into a giant, goofy smile, and for the first time in fifteen years, she felt something other than petrified of a dog.

"Wait till I tell the other kids I live next door to a

war hero and a marine dog." Teddy bounced on his toes. "Does Radar—?"

"Teddy, why don't you go inside?" she suggested again. "You can have that cupcake now and play some *Mario Kart* before setting the table for supper."

"But—but—"

"The offer of video-game time can be rescinded at any time." She gave her brother a warning look.

Radar whined as if he too was objecting. Gabriel Bishop shook his head at the dog. "Don't you start."

Despite the uncomfortable situation, Addie grinned at the dog's expression of dismay. She glanced up and her gaze met her neighbor's. Swallowing, she said, "Kids, huh?"

Gabriel's gaze held hers, and his mouth slowly curved upward until he was smiling at her. That simple gesture sent tingles skittering across her skin until he broke eye contact with a frown. But that smile… Talk about panty-melting.

Huh, maybe the dog wasn't the biggest threat to her peace of mind after all. But still, she'd feel a lot better if he owned one of those purse-sized pups instead of a big mean-looking one.

No, that wasn't fair. She spared a look at the dog. Yes, he was big, and that size alone was scary, but the way he was looking at Teddy bordered on adoration. How could she argue against that?

"Like I said, Radar and I are going inside, so you might want to listen to your sister."

The dog whined but trotted up the sidewalk to follow his master into the house, but not before giving Teddy one last doleful glance before the door shut.

Teddy heaved a put-upon sigh. "Can I have two cupcakes and play for two hours?"

Had Michelle even considered limiting Teddy's time watching television or playing video games? She should put her foot down, order him into the house. Letting him take advantage of her guilt wasn't healthy. "One cupcake now and another after supper."

A speculative gleam shone in his pale blue eyes. "What about *Mario Kart*? I don't have any homework."

"An hour and a half. And I don't want any arguments when I ask you to dry the dishes after supper."

He did a fist pump and ran ahead into the house. She glanced at the previously unoccupied side of the duplex—the one where that big dog now lived— and sighed. She'd work on setting stricter rules with Teddy. But first, she needed to get tough with herself and work on getting over her fear of dogs.

She would be doing it because overcoming it would be a step toward being the person Teddy needed her to be. All that self-improvement had nothing to do with those eyes flecked with brown, green and blue.

"Believe that and you'll be buying beachfront property in Arizona," she muttered and went into the house.

Once inside, she headed into the kitchen. Teddy had devoured a cupcake and left the plate on the counter, leaving not so much as a crumb behind. She set the dish in the sink and checked on him in his bedroom, where he was already playing his game. Shutting his door against the electronic noises, she pulled out her cell phone and made a call.

"I know why you're calling," Natalie said by way of greeting when she answered and added, "And I'm so sorry for not letting you know," before Addie could even speak.

Addie didn't pretend to misunderstand what Natalie was talking about. They had been friends ever since Addie had moved to Loon Lake. They'd bonded over single parenthood and formed their own supportive network of friends and single parents. "No apologies necessary. It's your place and I don't have any business putting my two cents in."

This wasn't about making Natalie feel guilty, so she injected lightness she wasn't feeling into her voice. "I was just surprised to learn I had a new neighbor."

"When I saw your name pop up on the caller ID, I realized I should have given you a heads-up. But since you're not upset, then I guess that means you've seen Gabriel Bishop."

"Oh, I've seen him." Not some of her finest moments. First, casting the new neighbor—an honest-to-goodness war hero, according to absolutely everyone who'd come into the library this past week—in the role of potential child snatcher. Then, instead of apologizing for her mistake, she'd stood there and spouted eye-color trivia at him. "But I meant no apologies necessary because it's your property and you can do what you want, rent to whomever you want."

What had gotten into her? She was usually more astute at reading people, but seeing Teddy with that big dog had flustered her, and all reasoning and logic had fled. She may feel justified in her reaction to seeing Teddy talking with a strange man, but letting it turn her into a shrew was unacceptable.

Natalie chuckled. "And the fact he's a hunk—and single, I might add—doesn't hurt, huh?"

Addie rolled her eyes even though her friend couldn't see her. She'd had it up to here with matchmaking. Her Harlequin ladies—the nickname she'd given the women who frequented the library and left with stacks of paperback romances—were on a mission to get her fixed up. Would they still feel the same if they knew her secret or would they redouble their efforts? She hadn't even confessed to Natalie that she was still a virgin at the ripe old age of twenty-two. It was nothing to be ashamed of, so she wasn't even sure herself why she hadn't told anyone.

Every week the ladies presented her with another choice. Loon Lake might be a small town, but its supply of single guys under the age of forty was starting to feel inexhaustible. Not that she didn't sometimes yearn for the closeness of having someone special to share her life with, but she wasn't going to be like their mother and bring a parade of unsuitable men into Teddy's life. She knew from childhood experience how confusing that could be. Of course, there'd been times when she'd been grateful that they'd disappeared because—

"Hey? You still there? I'm sorry if—"

"Stop apologizing!" Addie shook her head to clear the lingering thoughts from her past. "I'm not upset. Just…"

"Distracted by thoughts of a certain mouthwatering marine?" Natalie sighed. "If you weren't such a good friend, you'd have to fight me."

"Oh please." Addie tsk-tsked. "You are so in love with your husband you glow."

"Don't they say that about all pregnant women? I have a feeling Gabe could—"

"Will you cut that out?" Addie interrupted huffily but softened it with a laugh. Natalie and Des Gallagher were one of the happiest couples she knew, so all of this was Natalie's attempt at matchmaking. All the blissfully married couples she knew were as bad as those ladies at Colleen's Cut and Caboodle.

As if all those speculative glances cast in her direction by the library patrons each time Gabriel Bishop's name was mentioned weren't enough, now she had her good friend trying to matchmake. She needed to steer the conversation back toward her original purpose. Much safer territory. "I was surprised you rented it now, because you said you planned to get repairs and renovations done first. You mentioned talking to Ben McNamara about doing them."

"Oh, I did, and, hmm, you know Ben's hot and he's—"

"Stop it," Addie said before her friend could get carried away.

"Okay. Okay. I did ask Ben, but he's super busy with those Victorians on the other side of town. He gave me some names, but before I had a chance to talk to anyone else, I bumped into Brody and Mary at the Pic-N-Save."

Brody and Mary Wilson had transformed their farm on the outskirts of town into Camp Life Launch, a summer program mainly for children being raised in the foster care system. Although Addie's own time in the system had been brief, it had changed her, and she volunteered at the camp whenever she could. To repay her, the Wilsons allowed Teddy to attend some of the camp sessions to help Addie with childcare during the summer break from school.

"Anyway," Natalie continued, "Brody told me that Riley Cooper had told him that Gabe was looking for a place. The one Gabe was supposed to rent fell through when the owner's niece had a quickie wedding and decided she wanted it."

Addie snickered. "The Loon Lake grapevine in action."

"You got that right. Anyway, when I told Des, we decided to offer the place to Gabe. He was relieved to find another place, especially one that was partially furnished. He was so grateful, he agreed to do some of the renovation work along with any other issues that pop up. You'll have a maintenance person living on the premises."

"That's a good deal for both of you." Addie paced the kitchen, straightening the napkin holder and salt and pepper shakers on the small maple kitchen table before moving on to the living room.

"And not a bad deal for you since he's— Oh, I don't know—" Natalie heaved an exaggerated sigh before continuing, "Mr. Sex-on-a-Stick."

Good grief. Did everyone think she couldn't attract a man on her own? "I meant it's a good deal because it shortens Des's honey-do list."

"Which is why I am grateful for Gabe's willingness to take on the repairs and renovations. Ever since that national magazine did a feature on glass artists, Des has had more work than he can handle."

Natalie's husband was a gifted glass sculptor and had been a onetime, self-proclaimed scrooge until Natalie and her young son, Sam, burst into his life. Now he was a dedicated family man. Addie bent down and picked up a stray LEGO, placing it on the coffee table. At least she hadn't stepped on it. "But that's good, right? He deserves to have his talent recognized."

"Yes, it's very good. I'm just sorry I didn't warn you ahead of time Gabe was arriving. I meant to call you yesterday but fell asleep right after supper. I'd forgotten how tiring this first trimester is."

"Well, you just take care of yourself." Addie knew how excited her friends were about the pregnancy. And she was elated for them, but she couldn't help feeling envious and wondering if it would ever be her turn.

Natalie snorted. "No need to worry about that. Des is worse than a mother hen, and even Sam is waiting on me. I feel like a queen."

"As well you should," Addie told her, happy that Natalie had found love with a former naval aviator, whose career had been cut short when he'd received life-altering injuries. Her friend had lost her first husband in a tragic accident, which had also left her young son with a traumatic brain injury that had resulted in the boy being nonverbal.

They talked a few more minutes before ending with a promise of getting Teddy and Sam together soon. Natalie and Sam had lived on the other side of the duplex before she married Des, and the two boys had bonded over their love of LEGO bricks.

Back in the kitchen, she rooted around in a cupboard next to the refrigerator until she found a plastic storage container. She began frosting the cupcakes she'd left to cool while she picked up Teddy from the bus stop. She'd save some for her and Teddy, with the rest going to the monthly library meeting. The laminated sign Addie put on the door read Coffee & Conversation, but everyone in town referred to the meetings as Drinks & Drama. Small-town life's double-edged sword. People had your back in times of trouble but loved nothing more than to argue over mundane details of how to enact those plans.

As she frosted the cupcakes, her thoughts kept going back to her new neighbor. From what she could recall from the library patrons, Gabe had been awarded medals or ribbons or whatever it was that marines got for bravery on the battlefield. He'd said the dog wasn't military, but that didn't mean he hadn't done something heroic too. Maybe saved his life or something. Was that why he'd been so offended on the dog's behalf?

Great. She'd insulted two of America's finest in one day. *Nice going.* More snatches of this past week's gossip floated around in her head. She frowned. Not all of it had been flattering. Several ladies had lowered their voices and spoke of rowdy behavior and police involvement, but obviously nothing serious enough to keep him out of the military.

Retired schoolteacher Trudy Canterbury had clucked her tongue when recalling that Gabe had gotten married like "five minutes after graduating high school." Shaking her head, Trudy had added his wife had divorced him about "five minutes after he'd deployed."

Having your wife divorce you while you were off

fighting for your country couldn't have been easy. And now, thanks to her and her big mouth, she'd verified that he'd been the subject of town gossip.

Instead of putting the cover over the cupcakes, she set it aside and reached into one of the overhead cabinets and took down a plate. It was inexpensive melamine but one of her favorites. He probably wouldn't notice or care about the sunflowers or goldfinches, but using it made her feel better. Like an apology inside another apology.

She took out three cupcakes and arranged them on the plate. Did she even want to see Gabe Bishop again this soon? As if not seeing him was an option, considering he lived next door. It wasn't as if she could avoid him forever. And, knowing he nor the dog were a danger to Teddy, talking to him again wouldn't exactly be a hardship. Except that would also mean seeing Radar. But nothing in this life ever came without cost.

"Think of it as exposure therapy." Yeah, because that had worked so well in the past. She snorted. Maybe if she'd actually, really exposed herself…

Before she could change her mind, she grabbed her peace offering and went out the front door to the rectangular cement stoop the side-by-side duplexes shared. Throwing her shoulders back, she crossed the oh-so-short distance separating her from the dog.

Thankfully Teddy was in his room playing video games. Groveling would be embarrassing enough;

she didn't need an audience. She could set an example about taking responsibility by apologizing for her mistakes some other day. No doubt another teaching moment would arise in the next dozen or so years.

Her new neighbor's wooden door stood open, so she knocked on the glass of the storm door. Repairing or replacing the broken doorbell had been on Natalie's to-do list, so she didn't even bother with it. As she waited, she turned her head and glanced toward the house across the street in time to see the lace curtain in the front window fluttering. *Are you getting all this, Mrs. O?*

A widow in her eighties, Maureen O'Malley was one of the ladies who congregated weekly at Colleen's Cut and Caboodle. Come Thursday, you could bet Addie's visit to the new neighbor would be discussed as the regulars had their hair washed, styled and sprayed. Maureen was also the street's unofficial neighborhood watch. Nothing got past Mrs. O. What she didn't observe personally, she got from plying the gregarious mail carrier with her ricotta cheese cookies. Not many were strong enough to hold out against those frosted morsels of heaven.

Grinning, she turned back and— Yikes! The dog— Radar—was on the other side of the glass. He didn't bark or growl, just stood there watching her with an intenseness she found jarring. How long had he been there eyeing her? He seemed to be looking directly into her. Hey, at least he wasn't smacking his lips. Did he know how frightened she was? Heck, Mrs. O could probably see her knees knocking without the aid of her trusty binoculars.

The dog's nose began to twitch. Gulping, she did her best to control her reptilian brain reaction. Definitely flight—fight wasn't even on the menu.

Calm down. The dog was probably more interested in getting at the cupcakes than doing anything to her. Right? If she was lucky, the scent of the treats would mask the smell of her fear. Not that it mattered since dogs were also masters at reading body language. She groaned inwardly. Sometimes she hated her penchant for retaining bits of trivia.

"Did you know your sense of smell is around forty times greater than mine? Heck, you can probably pick out the individual ingredients even through this door. Red velvet cake batter has cocoa powder, vinegar or buttermilk, and it's the chemical reaction between them that—"

"Did you want something?"

Addie startled at the deep male voice and nearly dropped the plate. The cupcakes bounced and she clutched the dish tighter. She raised her gaze to Gabriel Bishop, who now stood behind his dog. He'd not only changed his clothes but shaved, and if his damp hair was any indication, he'd showered too. Whoa. He cleaned up nice. Maybe Natalie and the library ladies knew what they were talking about.

Down, girl. She bit her lower lip to contain the nervous laughter that bubbled up. "I...I..."

He scowled. "Did you need something, or did you come to give my dog a baking lesson?"

"Actually, we were talking about his sense of smell. Like I was telling him, dogs have up to three hundred million olfactory receptors in their noses and— Uh, well, never mind." Oh yeah, this wasn't embarrassing or anything. Her face hot enough to melt the cream cheese frosting on the cupcakes, she thrust out the plate. "Here, I came to give you these."

An emotion flickered across his face and disappeared before she could interpret it. The glower that replaced it was all too easy to read. Why couldn't she prevent trivia from dribbling out when she opened her mouth?

"Why?" he demanded, his straight brows clashing together.

"Why?" she echoed. Okay, embarrassment had tainted her presentation, but his reaction seemed out of proportion to her lack of grace. She shuffled her feet. "I wanted to apologize for my—" she swallowed "—earlier behavior. I—"

"Apology accepted. Was there anything else?" The dog whimpered and he gave Radar a pat on the head.

"You, uh, you don't want the cupcakes?" They weren't Maureen's coveted cookies, but they weren't bad. Teddy loved her red velvet cupcakes, and her little brother wasn't one to spare her feelings with spurious praise.

"I don't need chari— Uh, I mean, that's not necessary." He curled his palm around the edge of the inner wooden door and started to push. "The apology was sufficient."

"Oh. Well, um…" She took a step back as the door swung shut with a firm *thunk*. "Ohh-kaay."

She stood for a moment staring at the closed door. She stuck out her tongue, then called him a name that had her owing the swear jar another quarter— Ha! Considering Teddy had had to give up a quarter for saying "damn" while playing a game, she probably owed it some serious folding cash. A few more encounters like this with her new neighbor and she'd go broke. Of course, that wasn't exactly a long ride.

Chapter Three

Gabe stood in the center of the room and shifted his weight from one foot to the other, his gaze trained on the front window. She—what had the kid called her? Addie?—was crossing the street with her plate of cupcakes. Probably going to visit the curtain twitcher to report his rude behavior.

Radar made his I'm-not-happy-with-you noise, a cross between a woof and a growl, before ambling over to the window, his nails clicking on the hardwood floor. He stood panting, his breath fogging the glass, and watched their neighbor—or more likely those cupcakes she was carrying—sashay across the street.

"Yeah, I get it. I acted like an ass." Gabe sighed and rubbed the back of his neck.

"Bed," he ordered the dog.

Taking out your bad behavior on an innocent dog is beneath you.

Radar went to his dog bed and threw himself down. He lowered his head to his paws and breathed out a canine sigh. Gabe snort-laughed. That dog belonged in Hollywood.

"I don't know what you're complaining about. She can call them red velvet if she likes, but I could plainly see those cupcakes were chocolate. Dogs can't have chocolate."

Radar lifted his head, gave a low woof and lowered it again.

"Hey, I didn't make the rules."

No, but he could have been polite and accepted her offering. Instead, seeing her had slammed him back nearly two decades.

Back to that day when he'd opened the door of their trailer to his classmate Alan and Alan's mom. She'd been clutching a covered casserole dish, offered presumably because his pa had been injured on the job and unable to work.

He may have forgotten what food was in that dish, but branded on his brain was the woman's appalled expression as she'd glanced around the dilapidated trailer and junk-strewn yard. Her expression had morphed into pity when her gaze met Gabe's. What ten-year-old boy wanted to be pitied in front of his peers? That was the first time he'd experienced feeling ashamed of his circumstances, but not the last.

Seeing his new neighbor standing at his door with an offering had not only thrown him into his past but had him thinking serving his country hadn't changed a damn thing. As if she were saying he didn't belong on this neatly tended street. Of course, she'd been making a simple neighborly gesture.

Yeah, she looked like the do-gooder type. He rubbed a hand over his face. Closing the door on her hadn't been his finest moment. About on par with placing blame on the kid earlier. And ordering Radar into his dog bed. What was it about that woman that had him acting like a first-class jerk?

He knew the difference between apologizing or being neighborly and charity.

Shoving both hands into his back pockets, he watched as the curtain twitcher answered her door. The elderly woman smiled and nodded her head, obviously pleased to accept the cupcakes he'd refused. Damn, but he was a fool. The question was, what was he going to do to make up for his behavior? It wasn't this woman's fault he had issues—apparently unresolved ones—from his childhood.

"Got any ideas, dog? Short of only going out under cover of darkness to avoid her, what can I do? I signed a year's lease on this place." His financial situation wasn't dire. He still had a good chunk of combat pay squirreled away, but forfeiting a year's worth of rent wasn't possible. Not after all the dough he'd shelled out getting Radar here. Not that he begrudged a penny of that money.

The cupcakes disappeared inside the house along with the humans. Radar glanced up and woofed in response.

"Yeah, yeah, easy for you to say. You didn't hurt her feelings. You were happy enough to see her and her cupcakes."

He picked up one of the boxes he'd dragged in earlier and set it on the coffee table. Like the initial rental that had slipped through his fingers at the last minute, this apartment had come partially furnished. Loon Lake might celebrate him as a supposed war hero, but when it came to renting a furnished place to a guy with a seventy-five-pound dog, his status wasn't all that impressive.

Two days later, Gabe flattened the last cardboard storage box, glad the task was done at last. Unpacking had taken much longer than he'd expected. Mostly because he hadn't anticipated the flood of memories that had been in storage for so long. Those things included a few keepsakes from his mother, who had passed away from cancer when Gabe was six. After his pa's death during his second deployment to Afghanistan, he'd disposed of or donated most of the contents of their mobile home, except for small items he'd boxed up and put into storage. At that time, he'd vowed to deal with them in the future.

"Welcome to the future," he muttered, glancing over at a dozing Radar.

Surrounded by a bevy of new toys, the dog had supervised the proceedings from the comfort of his bed. Gabe shook his head at the sight. Looked like he needed to avoid the animal aisle at Pic-N-Save unless he was shopping for pet food.

Maybe he should stay out of local businesses entirely. He'd run into Sheriff Grayson Granger at the Pic-N-Save despite going first thing in the morning to avoid as many customers as possible. The sheriff had recognized him. No surprise there. The surprise was that the man had been genuinely pleased to see him, offering his hand.

Gabe had half expected the sheriff to slap on a pair of cuffs when he'd stuck out his own to shake. But Granger had pumped Gabe's hand and clapped him on the shoulder to welcome him home and thank him for such meritorious service.

While he appreciated the sheriff's forgiveness for youthful transgressions like underage drinking and some graffiti tagging, both of which he'd paid for. One with getting sick from drinking bourbon straight from the bottle and the other with having to clean up what he'd spray-painted. Looking back, he had to say he'd gotten off light. Not sure if it was a small-town thing or if his pa making him apologize to the sheriff had helped. But he hated all the war-hero nonsense. Since when did doing what he'd been trained to do count as heroism? He threw himself onto the sofa. If he'd been a true hero, he would have saved more than his own life. Radar would be with Tom and—

A wet nose nudged his hand. Radar whimpered and rested his head on Gabe's knee. The dog looked up at him with adoration, not a hint of reproach. Sighing, he rubbed Radar's ears. Why was everyone so willing to forgive him? What had he done in his life to deserve such magnanimous absolution? He'd escaped a teenage marriage by joining the marines and he'd literally escaped death in Afghanistan by winning a coin toss.

Radar's ears twitched and he broke away. Trotting to the door, he sniffed around the bottom. Gabe may not be able to rattle off numbers regarding the dog's olfactory receptors, but he did know Radar recognized the person on the other side, because his tail was working like a metronome. Radar sat and stared at the door in anticipation. Finally someone knocked.

Sighing again, he dropped the flattened cardboard on the pile and went to check. With careful timing, he'd managed to avoid his neighbors since shutting the door in the woman's lovely face. Several times he'd thought about going over to apologize, but he hadn't gotten past the thinking stage.

Maybe this would be his opportunity. Drawing a

deep breath, he pulled open the door, vowing to use the manners he'd been taught.

Teddy stood on the other side of the glass. Okay, he wasn't disappointed. Nope. He'd only hoped it was her so he could apologize for his boorish behavior. Yup, that explained it.

As soon as he unlatched the storm door, Radar pushed his nose out. Gabe made a grab for his collar, but the dog was faster and wriggled through the space, showering the kid with sloppy kisses.

"It's so good to see you again. I missed you so much," Teddy told the slobbering dog.

"Yeah, it's been a whole two days," Gabe said. You'd think by the way they greeted one another that the pair had been cruelly separated for months instead of days. What had gotten into Radar?

Teddy lifted his head. "Huh?"

"Nothing. Forget it," Gabe said. It wasn't the kid's fault he was in a bad mood. He'd regretted acting like such an ass to his pretty neighbor. He didn't want to subject her brother to the same treatment. What harm would it have caused to have taken her cupcakes? Instead, he'd been petty.

Teddy hugged Radar, who hadn't stopped squirming and nearly knocked the giggling kid onto his butt on the cement steps outside the door.

Great. The last thing he needed was to have to explain scrapes or injuries to the boy's sister. No telling how she'd react. Especially if Radar was to blame.

And it would be his fault for repaying her apology with rudeness.

"Sit," he ordered Radar before dealing with the boy.

Teddy scrunched up his face and glanced down. "Here? But…"

Gabe bit the inside of his cheek. "I was talking to Radar."

Radar obeyed, but ripples of excitement continued to course through his entire body.

"Wow. He listens real good. I'll be sure and tell Addie." The boy dropped to his knees and put his arms around the dog. "She keeps saying dogs are too expensive. I said we just won't take it to the vet, but she says that's not the way good parents should behave," the boy parroted his sister.

Gabe rubbed a hand across his mouth. The kid did a pretty good imitation of Addie.

Teddy rested his cheek against Radar's fur. "I think she just doesn't like dogs too much."

The movement caused the sweatshirt sleeve to pull up and expose those scars marring the child's hands and wrists. Yeah, definitely burn scars. Gabe grimaced. Not fresh, but the kid couldn't be more than six or seven. How did—? He pushed those thoughts aside. Not his business. And he wasn't making it his business either. He needed to get his own life in order, not get involved in someone else's.

Gabe glanced down at the boy. He really shouldn't

be encouraging drop-in visits. "Was there a reason why you came?"

"Oh yeah…" The kid sprang up and straightened his shoulders. "Hello, Mr. Bishop. I'm Teddy from next door. I tol' Addie you already know that, but she said I needed to be polite and that maybe it will rub off on you. Uh—" He scratched his scalp. "But I think I wasn't s'pose to say that last part, because she said it real low and I'll bet she doesn't know I heard her. You won't tell her I tol' you, will you?"

Gabe coughed into his hand. He didn't want to hurt the kid's feelings by openly laughing. Something about this kid made his chest tighten, like the time he'd had pneumonia. The past couldn't be changed, so he had tried hard not to dwell on all that emotional stuff over the years. But if he'd survived, his own son would have been only a year or two older than Teddy, so comparisons were inevitable. Would he have been a chatterbox? Or a dog lover? Would he and Tracy still be together?

"…to ask if you had a wrench we could borrow. She also said to just come back if you said no or shut the door in my face. But I said you wouldn't do that. You wouldn't, would you?"

Gabe rubbed a hand over his chest. To be honest, closing the door on the kid had been his first instinct. Something about Teddy and Addie set off alarm bells. Like getting involved with either would drag him further than he wanted to go. Not only was she young, but responsible for a kid. He doubted she was out for a good time.

"For starters, you can call me Gabe." *Yeah, that's a big step toward not getting involved.* "Now, did your sister say why she needs a wrench?"

"She's trying to get the water turned off under the kitchen sink."

The boy was busy petting Radar and telling his newfound friend how much he'd missed him, so Gabe prompted him. "Why is she doing that?"

"Because the handle thing on top broke." Teddy buried his fingers in Radar's fur. "It was real cool. I heard Addie yell a bad word, so I paused my game and ran into the kitchen. I was gonna make sure she put money in the jar, but water was spraying up and…" The boy paused to draw in a breath. "Addie was getting wet trying to stop it, so instead I got the bucket she uses to wash the floor, and she put it over the water. It didn't stop it, but now it's going into the sink instead of into the air."

Gabe scooped his keys off the small table in the hall. That sounded urgent and like something he could help with. That was even better than a simple apology. "I have a toolbox in my Jeep. I'll get it."

"Addie was so mad I didn't even tell her she owed the swear jar. Good thing the clipboard lady wasn't there today. I heard Addie tell Sam's mom that the lady scares her, and she has to be careful what she says in front of her."

Gabe had no idea what the kid was talking about but nodded as if he did. He stood at the open door and pressed the key fob to unlock his Jeep sitting in the driveway.

Teddy looked up at him. His light blue eyes seemed to be searching for reassurance. "I thought being an adult meant you didn't have to be afraid of stuff like that anymore. What about you? Were you afraid when you were in the war?"

Oh kid, don't look to me for answers. Any answers to anything. Gabe clenched his jaw. How had their simple conversation morphed into this? Yeah, he needed to put some distance between him and the child. And his sister. She was obviously responsible for her brother and needed someone she could rely on. His divorce proved he wasn't reliable. "Why don't we save this discussion for another time?"

"Why are people always saying that?"

"Because right now your sister needs help getting the water shut off."

He definitely didn't want to get involved in their family drama, but he could take a look at her leak. It was part of his agreement with the landlord and had nothing to do with his neighbor's bright blue eyes or those freckles begging to be kissed.

"Can Radar come with us?"

"Did you say there's water on your kitchen floor?"

"Just a little from before we got the bucket over it."

"Even so. I don't think we need Radar adding to

your sister's troubles by having a dog tramp through wet floors." Gabe pointed to Radar. "Radar, bed."

The water was a good excuse, but he also agreed with Teddy that his sister didn't like dogs much. Or maybe just his pet. Or him. But that was okay because he wasn't getting involved.

Teddy stuck his bottom lip out in a serious pout and Radar began to whine. Damn, but those two were killin' him. How had he gone from being the sergeant dubbed tough as a woodpecker's lips to pushover in record time? And what happened to keeping his distance and not getting involved?

"How about you two play outside? I have a tennis ball you can throw. Radar likes to play fetch."

"Really?" The boy's face lit up. "Hear that, Radar? We can play ball."

Radar woofed his agreement.

Gabe shook his head. You would've thought he'd promised to take the kid to a theme park, but it felt strangely satisfying to make the kid happy with such a simple gesture. The strange tightness in his chest had eased and he couldn't help grinning when he retrieved one of Radar's tennis balls.

"Um…" Teddy made a face. "Maybe I should tell Addie first."

"I'll let her know," Gabe said and handed Teddy a ball. "You'll just be here in the front yard."

"Yeah, she forgets I'm not a baby anymore." He ran down the steps but Radar stayed in the same spot, looking at Gabe as if seeking permission to follow.

"At ease," he said, and the dog tore off after Teddy and the ball. That had been one of the commands Tom had taught Radar. Gabe smiled, but the memory was bittersweet.

He watched for a moment while Teddy threw the ball. The kid could use some pitching lessons. Did he not have anyone to toss the ball with and give him pointers on holding it? Maybe he could— No. None of his business. He opened the back of his gray Jeep, then grabbed his tool chest and the cardboard box of assorted fixtures Natalie had given him.

He'd find out what was wrong with his neighbor's faucet and fix or replace it because that was the neighborly thing to do. After that, he'd stick to his side of the duplex and mind his own business.

Gabe let himself into Teddy's side of the duplex and glanced around. The living room was the same size as his and had similar-looking, hand-me-down furniture. Had he ever lived in a place with brand-new pieces?

He didn't know Teddy and Addie's family situation, but taking responsibility for a younger sibling couldn't be easy. As the product of a single-parent household from the age of six himself, he knew it could be a struggle.

Unsure of his welcome after their last encounter,

he shifted the box under his arm, gripped his tool chest tighter and headed for the kitchen. He hefted both onto the scarred wood of the table and opened his mouth to announce his presence, but nothing came out. He forgot why he was here. His attention was riveted on the heart-shaped butt sticking out from the open cabinet under the sink as she knelt on her hands and knees.

"Well? Did he have a wrench?" she inquired and started to shimmy backward. "Teddy?"

Gabe swallowed and found his voice. "He did, but if the shut-off valve is stuck, you need Channellock pliers, not a wrench."

She made a startled noise and got up before clearing the cabinet. He winced at the noise her head made when making contact with the wood but couldn't prevent a grin at the curse words she uttered.

"Better not let your brother hear you use that language. He seems pretty keen on that swear jar."

"It's on the honor system," she muttered distractedly and scooted out the rest of the way and scrambled to her feet, facing away from him as she grabbed a towel and wiped her face.

Good thing she had her back to him. He figured it was best not to let her see him grinning. He was probably in enough hot water with his attractive neighbor as it was.

He wiped off the grin and cleared his throat. "What exactly happened?"

"The faucet has been dripping, and when I tried to turn it off a bit tighter, the handle snapped off. It was like the Old Faithful geyser in here."

Opening the tool chest, he lifted the tray out and set it aside. The pliers would be on the bottom along with a small can of WD-40. His pa might not have noticed what a mess their yard was, but he'd kept his tools in pristine condition. "That's what Teddy said. Did the shut-off valve break too, or is it just stuck?"

She folded the towel and put it on the counter. "Stuck. After what had just happened, I was careful not to force it too much."

"Good. It should just be a case of loosening it. I'll spray it first with some, um…" He glanced up as she turned around and had to clamp his mouth shut around what would most likely be an embarrassing sound.

Her T-shirt was soaked and plastered to her chest, giving him a peek at what appeared to be a pink lace bra. Pink was suddenly his new favorite color.

As an officer and a gentleman, he should look away, turn his back, something. Except he was no longer an officer.

And obviously not a gentleman either.

Yeah, he should look away. He really, really should. He should be ashamed of himself. He really, really should.

"Some what?" she asked, using her fingers to explore the back of her head and pulling the shirt even tighter across her chest.

Her puzzled gaze met his while he was still doing the whole fish thing of opening and closing his mouth.

"You—you, uh…" He swallowed and waved a hand in her general direction.

She glanced down at herself and turned beet red. "Yes, well, if you, uh, if you'll excuse me, I'll just go and dry off."

He nodded like a bobblehead doll and called himself all kinds of jerk as she turned and fled. Damn. His teenage self had had smoother moves. And look what that had gotten him. He and Tracy Harris couldn't keep their hands off one another. So much so he found himself married and anticipating fatherhood at eighteen. He cursed and reached for the pliers. Turning back toward the sink, he spotted a clear glass jar with a white screw-on lid. It held an impressive array of coins and a few bills. *It's on the honor system.* He patted his front pocket for loose change and dropped it in. With a snorted laugh, he hunkered down to get under her sink.

Chapter Four

On her way to her bedroom, Addie stopped to grab a towel. Safely alone, she peeled off her wet clothes and draped them over the hamper in the corner. The loose change she'd shoved into her jeans' pocket at the Pic-N-Save fell out and hit the floor with a jingle.

She stooped to retrieve the coins. Those belonged in Teddy's jar. Despite referring to it as Teddy's, she'd instituted the whole thing as much for herself as for him. As if to prove a point, most of the money in it had come from her.

Even though she no longer needed that tough outer shell since she'd left her mother's world behind, some habits were hard to break. The swear jar was christened the day she'd gotten called to the school for Teddy's own inappropriate language.

Setting the coins on the dresser, she used the towel to dry off and put on a more sedate white bra. Not that it mattered now. She'd already given the sexy new neighbor a show. Why had she let Natalie talk her into buying such racy underwear that time they'd taken a girls-only shopping trip a few months ago? It wasn't as if there was anyone but her to see it. At least, no one until today. She hurriedly finished dressing in dry clothes.

Catching her reflection in the mirror above the dresser, she frowned. It was her day off from the library, so she hadn't bothered with any makeup. Maybe that was a good thing since she'd just taken an unexpected shower at the kitchen sink. Still… What was the harm in a little lip gloss?

Plenty. After the show you put on, do you really want to go back in there looking like some femme fatale? What sort of message would that send?

Her? A femme fatale for wearing lip gloss? Shaking her head at her silliness, she hurried back to the kitchen before she gave in to the urge to drag out her neglected stash of makeup. She was supposed to be concentrating on the upcoming hearing in family court, not on the hot former marine next door. Growing up, she'd never been anyone's priority, and she didn't want that for Teddy.

The men in her mother's life always came before

her children. Eventually, getting high came even before the men, unless they were keeping her supplied. So her children were ranking a distant third.

She stopped short in the doorway when she saw legs and scuffed tan boots sticking out from under the sink. It took her a moment to realize the water was no longer gushing from the broken faucet. "Ooh, you fixed it."

As a distraction from thinking about what was attached to those long limbs, she dropped her Pic-N-Save change into the jar. There was a jingle as the coins dropped.

He scooted out from under the sink and stood, wiping his hands on the dish towel she'd left on the counter. "I got the water turned off. The fixing part comes next."

"At least you stopped Old Faithful."

He hitched his chin toward the empty bucket she'd overturned onto the spurting faucet handle. It had been redirecting the water into the sink. She'd even placed a can of beans on top of the bottom of the bucket to keep it in place. "Inventive solution."

"Actually, Teddy suggested it. Probably saw it on television." She grinned. "Who says watching cartoons is a waste of time?"

"Not me." He chuckled and folded the towel.

Her stomach flip-flopped at the way his eyes crinkled in the corners when he laughed. Afraid her reaction to him might show in her voice, she cleared her throat before speaking. "Thank you for coming to my rescue."

"It was my pl—" he started and stopped. Swallowing, he continued, "Uh, just keeping up part of the bargain."

Her face grew warm. Like shutting the door in her face, was he deliberately shutting down any friendly overtures? He couldn't think she'd staged the wet T-shirt incident, could he? "Well, I still appreciate it. I guess I'll need to pick up some new faucet handles."

"That won't be necessary."

"You're not going to tell me you walk around with replacement faucet handles."

"Okay, I won't tell you." Laughing, he opened the box on the table.

"But—but…" she sputtered. His deep laugh had sent ripples straight to her tummy, leaving her incapable of coherent speech.

He poked around in the box. "Actually, Natalie gave me a box of supplies she had for her planned upgrades of this place. So, I can exchange them right now, if that works for you."

"It does, and Teddy will be relieved. He had a fit one time when I filled a water bottle from the faucet in the bathroom." Good Lord. What was wrong with her? Why did she just say something so inane? It wasn't as if they shared anything more than an address.

Good grief, what must he think of her?

"You made him drink bathroom water?" He glanced up and stared at her, eyes wide. He shook his head. "How could you?"

"Not you too! It comes out of the faucet just like—" His laughter interrupted her and she shook her head. "I almost fell for that."

"Sorry. I couldn't resist." He pulled some items from the box and went back to the sink.

She fiddled with the neck of her sweatshirt. Maybe she should have been more receptive to those ladies' matchmaking attempts—then she'd have had more practice with flirting. Was that even what they were doing? Flirting? Or was she misreading what had just happened?

She dropped her hand. "Speaking of Teddy, I should go check on him. He must've gone straight back to his video game. Now that Sam has moved, he doesn't have anyone to play outside with."

He turned back toward her. "Then you'll be pleased to know he's in the yard playing fetch with Radar."

Some guardian she made. She was in here flirting, thinking of only herself, and hadn't given a thought to Teddy's whereabouts. "You left him outside—all alone—with that dog?"

"That dog's name is Radar and he's mine." He scowled at her.

Heat flared in her cheeks. She opened her mouth, but he continued before she could form an apology.

"Like I said before. Radar isn't a threat to Teddy… God knows why, but they seem to have developed a sudden and deep connection."

She had trouble getting enough air into her lungs. In her rational mind, she knew he spoke the truth. Just because the dog scared the wits out of *her*, that didn't mean he was a menace. She could probably be confronted with Lassie and be just as afraid. "I can see that but—"

"In case you hadn't noticed, your brother is not a toddler needing constant supervision while playing in the front yard."

He had no idea what could happen when a child was left unsupervised. Unfortunately, she knew all too well. She pointed toward the window over the sink. "And in case *you* hadn't noticed, there's all sorts of things out there that could hurt him."

He glanced out the window, then back to her. "Like what? Grass stains? Sorry. I'm not seeing it. It's a peaceful street."

"You have no idea how unsafe the world can…" Her voice trailed off when he raised an eyebrow. Her shoulders drooped. Well, didn't she look like a shallow fool? How many tours had he served in a war zone? *Good going, Addie.* "Right. Afghanistan."

He ripped open the seal on a small box. "You have every right to be concerned for his safety. I've seen his scars."

"I should have been there." The words were out

before she could stop them. Her mind whirring, she studied her feet. What was she doing? Why would she admit such a painful feeling to a virtual stranger?

Because their mother had been clean since Teddy's birth, Addie had accepted a college scholarship and moved away. Unfortunately, without Addie's help, Michelle couldn't cope and fell back into old habits. Addie should never have trusted her enough to leave. But she had, and Michelle had left a pan of boiling hot water in the sink and Teddy had tried to sail his toy boat in it when their mother left the room.

He cleared his throat. "Even when we are, sometimes we can't prevent the bad stuff from happening."

Her head popped up at his quietly spoken words, and her gaze collided with his and held. She saw what was probably reflected in her own eyes. Guilt. Regret. Sadness. No other words were spoken. They weren't needed, but she did wonder what memory had caused those emotions to appear in his eyes.

Although they were almost strangers, she sensed something meaningful had passed between them. As if they were letting the other see a piece of themselves they didn't normally show the rest of the world.

The refrigerator's ice maker dropped cubes into the bin in the freezer, breaking the silence.

"I didn't mean to—"

"I shouldn't have—"

"How about this?" He held out his hand. "Hi, my name is Gabe Bishop, and I'm your new neighbor."

She looked at his hand for a second, then grabbed it and shook. "Nice to meet you, Gabe. I'm Addie Miller, and I live here with—"

"Addie! Hey, Addie." A door banged, followed by sneakers slapping on the floor. Teddy appeared in the kitchen, wide-eyed, disheveled and panting. "Radar just saved my life."

"What? What are you talking about?" She rushed to her brother and hunkered down in front of him, checking him for signs of fresh injury. "Are you okay?"

"I threw the ball and it went into the street and—"

"Oh, Teddy, you didn't." She couldn't shut down the gut-churning thoughts of what might have happened. He was standing in front of her—unharmed—and yet her mind insisted on playing scenarios that would have sent Teddy to the ER.

"Someone want to tell me what's going on?" Gabe asked, glancing between them.

"Radar ran right in front and tripped me," Teddy finished.

Gabe set the new faucet handle next to the sink. "I'm going to venture a guess and say you attempted to run into the street after the ball."

She was her mother's daughter, responsibilities forgotten whenever a man was on the scene. She tugged Teddy closer. "Twelve percent of all traffic deaths in this country involve pedestrians," she stated by rote but gave a squirming Teddy a fierce hug.

"Yuck, Addie," Teddy protested. "I'm too old for PDA."

Addie wasn't sure if she should laugh or cry. "How do you even know what that means?"

"I get around," Teddy said as he took a step back and shrugged. "I know stuff."

Gabe snickered, covering it with a cough. Addie glanced toward the sounds, but instead of seeing him, Radar filled her field of vision. The dog sat patiently next to his owner. Her heart began beating against her chest as if trying to escape her rib cage. Thoughts crashed inside her head. The dog. In her kitchen. In her space.

She inhaled. *That dog* had protected Teddy, she argued with herself. Determined, she swallowed back her fear and forced herself to look Radar in the eyes. "Thank you, Radar, for protecting Teddy."

The dog thumped his tail and looked up at Gabe, who rubbed the fur between the large ears. "Good job."

She turned her attention to Gabe, not easy with the animal in the room. Gabe seemed to be studying her. Had he guessed her secret? Yeah, it wasn't exactly a big mystery. She wasn't sure if it was embarrassment or guilt that made her guard her secret.

Embarrassment because she was an adult afraid of a dog. Yes, in certain circumstances she might be justified in being afraid of a dog like Radar, but this wasn't one of those. And guilt because her fear prevented Teddy from getting a fervently wished-for pet of his own.

Her fear stemmed from being bitten as a child. But she was now an adult and should be able to conquer her phobias. An incident from her youth shouldn't be ruling her life as a grown woman. Even the physical scars had begun to fade with time.

Gabe raised an eyebrow in inquiry. Oh yeah, he knew, but he also seemed to be asking her if she was okay. She nodded and managed a bit of bravado with a thin smile. Satisfied, he turned his attention back to attaching the new faucet handle. He wasn't going to out her in front of Teddy.

"Can Radar and I go back out and play? I promise I won't run into the road," Teddy said, reaching out to give Radar a pat on the head. "And besides, it was old Mr. Peterson driving. Even you say turtles could beat him down the street. And you never say anything bad about anyone."

Good thing, or it would be all over Loon Lake in a heartbeat. She made a mental note to not only curb her swearing but not to engage in any gossip. At least around her little brother.

A tingling sensation swept up the back of her neck. How was it that Teddy heard all the stuff he wasn't meant to and yet appeared to be tone deaf to the things she told him directly? Like not to talk to strangers or dart into the street. How was she supposed to keep him safe if her cautions went in one ear and out the other?

"I shouldn't have said that about sweet Mr. Peterson. Don't repeat it to anyone. Please." What sort of things did he spill to the social worker? Or the court-appointed advocate? As if she didn't have enough to worry about. "How can you play without a ball?"

"Oh yeah, I forgot." His shoulders slumped and he patted Radar. "I'm sorry for losing your ball."

"Maybe you should also apologize to Mr. Gabe."

Gabe shook his head. "That's not necessary."

"I didn't mean to lose the ball. Honest." Teddy pushed his lower lip out. "I can go right now and—"

"No, you can't. You stay out of the road. Next time it might be a less sedate driver." She shuddered to think what could have happened. She glanced at Radar and silently thanked him again.

"Don't worry about the ball. There's plenty more where that came from." Gabe gathered up his tools. "I'm going to test turning on the water. Then Radar and I are going home."

"Ooh, can I watch?" Teddy stopped petting Radar to gaze up at Gabe. "It was really cool before, with water squirting everywhere."

"Yeah, real cool." Addie rolled her eyes, but secretly she had to admit it had all turned out okay in the end.

Yeah, you can say that because you got to see Gabe at work.

Teddy puffed out his chest. "I was the one who came up with using a bucket on the water."

"That's what your sister said. Very clever. Put her there, sport." Gabe fist-bumped with a beaming Teddy. "Do you want to test the faucet?"

Teddy did a little bounce. "Can I? Really? Did you hear that, Addie?"

Seeing the excitement and admiration on her brother's face at such a mundane task gave her a fleeting moment of anxiety. Lots of boys grew up to be well-adjusted, successful men in female-only households. Plus, he had Des Gallagher and Brody Wilson in his life. True, her friends' husbands were busy with their own growing families, but they definitely made excellent role models.

Teddy grunted as he leaned over the sink to turn the water on. "It works. Look. It works."

She nodded. "I see that. We need to thank Mr. Gabe."

"Thanks, Mr. Gabe. Maybe now you could show me how to fix stuff so I can help too."

Gabe was at a loss for words. The earnest pleading in Teddy's expression as he looked up tugged at something Gabe had kept buried deep inside. And it stung. This kid shouldn't be looking up to him, and yet the admiration in his gaze filled a spot he hadn't even known was empty.

He'd been about Teddy's age when his pa had allowed him to help around their home. He could almost taste the pride he'd felt when Pa had put that flat-head screwdriver into his open palm. He could still feel the smooth wood of the handle, the indentations where his father's initials had been carved into the wood.

"Mr. Gabe?"

Gabe blinked as he came back to the present.

"Teddy, why don't you go to your room? You can finish playing your game before supper."

"But…"

Radar leaned against his leg and Gabe winced. Obviously, his silence had spoken volumes, and it probably said something he hadn't meant to relay. Hurting the boy's feelings was the last thing he'd intended. He inhaled deeply, hoping his voice didn't betray his riotous feelings. "Next time I do a job that requires an extra set of hands, you'll be the first person I think of."

"Really?"

Radar snuffled and Gabe laughed. "You're right, Radar. Teddy will make a great helper."

Addie smiled, but it didn't reach her eyes. Did she think he was just placating her brother? More important, was that what he was doing? Saying something to make the kid happy, then not intending to follow through? He made a mental note to find something he could ask Teddy to help with. "Here. We'll shake on it. How's that? Radar, shake hands with Teddy."

Radar offered his paw to Teddy, who was beaming as he took it. "Wow. That's so cool. Radar shook hands with me. Did you see that, Addie?"

"I saw. That was really cool," she said, her tone infused with a sense of wonder.

How many times a day did Teddy say that? He'd barely spent any time with the boy, but he'd bet this was a pattern with him. And yet she was able to react without spoiling his enthusiasm.

He needed to remember he wasn't in a position to get involved with anyone, and especially not a woman who was responsible for a child. But it was that dedication to her brother that drew him to her. He swallowed. He was finding way too many things to admire about Addie Miller.

"Did you teach him to shake hands?"

Teddy's question broke into Gabe's musings, and he shook his head. "Wish I could take credit. A good buddy of mine, Tom, taught him just about everything he knows."

"If your friend taught Radar all that stuff, how come Radar lives with you? Did he teach him for you? Like at school? Why doesn't Radar live with him?"

Because life and death came down to a flip of

a coin and a moment in time I'd give my life to go back and change.

"Tom died, so now I take care of Radar." He hoped that would satisfy the boy.

Radar whined as if he'd understood the reference to Tom.

Oh man, why had he mentioned Tom? He should've taken credit and left it at that. He suspected a simpler approach with Teddy worked best.

Judging by his scars and how his earlier questions alluded to fear, Teddy must've experienced some of life's ugliness. He had no idea what Teddy's mother suffered from, but the kid hadn't had an easy life. And he suspected neither had his sister. Was that why, even in a town like Loon Lake, the woman was so protective?

Teddy bent down to hug Radar. "I'm sorry the man who taught you all that cool stuff died. Our mom didn't die, but she kept getting sick, so I live with Addie now. Just like you live with Mr. Gabe now. It's gonna be okay. You'll see."

Damn, but that kid, whom he barely knew, had the ability to scrape him raw emotionally. If he wasn't careful, these two would be drawing him in, and he sure as hell had no business going there. Even if she didn't have responsibility for her brother, Addie definitely looked like the forever type. And he was obviously missing the gene that made him a good bet for the long haul. Just ask the Marine

Corps. When he'd joined, he'd intended on being a lifer but got burned out after a dozen and didn't re-enlist. He'd promised his ex-wife a lifetime too and that promise had ended in less than two.

"Mr. Gabe?"

Gabe blinked and refocused his attention. He couldn't help but smile at the expectant expressions not only on the boy but Radar too. "Yes?"

"Can Radar and me play again sometime?"

"I think Radar would like that," Gabe said, and Radar woofed his agreement. "But we have to make sure it's okay with your sister."

Teddy balanced on his toes and gave his sister a pleading look. "Can I, Addie? Can I?"

Radar's attention was fixed on Addie too, as if understanding his stake in the conversation. But that wasn't possible, was it? And what the hell happened to not getting involved? Between the boy and Radar, he was being sucked in.

She sighed. "As long as Gabe doesn't mind."

Ah, so she'd caught how he'd said Radar would like it and left himself out of the equation. What was wrong with him when he was around her? Why did she bring out his inner rudeness?

Feeling everyone's gaze on him, he said, "I don't mind."

Teddy scuffed his toe on the vinyl flooring. "And, uh, maybe I could, like, help you again next time you work on something?"

"Teddy, why don't you go finish your video game? I'm sure we've wasted enough of Mr. Gabe's time."

Yeah, she'd caught his less-than-enthusiastic response to Teddy playing with Radar. Snapping his fingers at the dog, he opened the door to the backyard. "Patrol."

Radar hesitated and Gabe nudged him out the door. "You can play with Teddy tomorrow."

Teddy hadn't said a word, but his shoulders were hunched forward as he started to leave the room.

Gabe heaved a sigh. "Teddy, wait."

The marines had taught him better. So had his pa. He had to remedy the situation, needed to figure out how to live next door to Addie. He was a grown-ass man and a former marine, so why was it so hard to keep his reaction to his new neighbor under control?

Chapter Five

Gabe scratched his chin. Did he want to do this? Not really, but his reluctance to get involved faded away when confronted with the hopeful expression on the boy's face.

"I may have something tomorrow, if Addie says it's fine. Come over when you get home from school. Okay?"

"Really?" The boy's eyes widened, and he turned to his sister. "Can I, Addie? Can I?"

Addie nodded and the boy grinned from ear to ear. "Gee, thanks, Mr. Gabe. What about maybe to-night? I—"

"You have Cub Scouts tonight. Remember?"

The boy's shoulders drooped again. "Oh yeah."

"You like Cub Scouts, and Mr. Gabe already invited you for after school tomorrow," Addie said.

The boy gave him an assessing look. "You won't forget by then? Sometimes grown-ups forget so they don't have to do stuff."

"I won't forget." In his peripheral vision, he saw Addie move closer to Teddy. Gabe put a hand to his chest. "You have my word on it."

That seemed to satisfy the boy and he loped off to his room.

"Sorry about that," she said after Teddy had left. "That was sweet of you, but I'll understand if you don't want him getting in your way. I can make some excuses if—"

"I'll keep my word." Did she think he'd string the kid along? Why not? He hadn't exactly been Mr. Congeniality around her. She opened her mouth and he rushed in before she could say anything. "As long as you don't think I'm taking advantage of him if I let him help me wash my Jeep."

"That sounds perfect," she said with a nod. "He can't get into too much trouble with that."

He huffed out a laugh. "Obviously you've never seen a preadolescent boy wash a car."

"You may have a point." She grinned, carving deep dimples into her cheeks. "But thank you anyway."

Trying not to embarrass himself over those dimples, he shrugged. Where was all this cool resolve he'd promised himself a few minutes ago? Talk about running hot and cold. No wonder she expected him to weasel out of a promise to Teddy. "Hey. I'm the one getting the free labor."

Her blue eyes softened as she continued to smile. Gabe swallowed a groan, starting a mental list why getting involved with Addie was a bad idea. Over a decade had passed, but except for the more stable financial standing, he wasn't in a much better place than when he'd married Tracy. He was approaching thirty now, and yet here he was, back to figuring out what to do with his life, picturing the community-college brochure waiting for him on the kitchen counter. He still wasn't convinced his decision not to reenlist after Tom's death had been the right one. Maybe cutting and running was his MO when things got tough. If so, then he had no business in a relationship. With anyone.

"And, just so you know, I wasn't doubting your word. It's just that Teddy has not always been able to rely on the things people have said to him."

Her words broke into his musings. A sudden urge to know more about her came over him. After all, he wanted them to be friendly neighbors. Yep, that was it. "And what about you?"

"Me?" Her head snapped back. "I have always tried to—"

"No! I said it wrong." *Way to go, Gabe.* "What I meant was, do people break their promises to you?"

He began packing up his tools before he could ask more stupid questions and get in deeper with the lovely neighbor, his lack of control being what it was.

"I'm not seven."

His head snapped up. "No, you're not."

Was that his voice? It sounded more like a rusty rasp, thanks to his memory of exactly how adult she was playing in his head. In vivid detail and bright saturated colors on a continuous loop.

She blushed, making her freckles stand out in contrast. He had never thought he'd be attracted to freckles. Or dimples. Or women who blushed.

"Well, I don't know how to thank you for coming to my rescue." She cleared her throat. "I baked another batch of red velvet cupcakes, if I can tempt you."

She was tempting all right, but he ordered himself not to go there. *Concentrate on the cupcakes.*

"Red velvet? Are those the ones with chocolate and—" he tried not to make a face "—vinegar?"

A flash of humor crossed her features. "Don't say it like that. The acidity of the vinegar or buttermilk is what causes a chemical reaction with the cocoa powder and gives the cake a reddish color. But you have to be sure the pH balance hasn't been neutralized like with Dutch-processed cocoa powder or the reaction won't occur. Anyway, I used buttermilk instead of vinegar because I like the tangy taste paired with the mild chocolate and vanilla and…"

Her voice had trailed off.

"Gotcha." Someone throw him a life preserver! He was drowning in those dimples.

"Sorry. I'm a librarian." Now she looked more embarrassed than amused. "Information is my game."

He wiggled his eyebrows, hoping to put her at ease again. "So, conversations with you will be like auditioning for *Jeopardy!*?"

"Look at you, putting your answer in the form of a question," she said.

"And you're a fountain of information." He was rewarded with another blushing smile. A sense of humor. He liked that. *Are you sure you want to find out even more things about her?* chided an inner voice.

"More like a babbling brook of useless trivia." She laughed.

Gabe's gut wasn't the only part of his anatomy that reacted to her expression and the sound of her clear, sweet laughter.

"So, would you like some?"

A breathless "Oh yeah" slipped out before he could prevent it. But judging from her puzzled reaction, they were on totally different wavelengths.

Now it was his turn to blush. At least, judging from the warmth rising up his neck to his cheeks, he figured he was. What was he? Seventeen again? Hell, he— Oops.

He hitched his chin at the swear jar. "You said that was honor system?"

"'Fraid so."

He dug into his pocket for some coins, found none and pulled out his wallet. "You were talking cupcakes, right?"

"Of course. What did you think I meant?"

"Cupcakes," he said but opened his wallet and stuck a bill in the jar. "And, yes, please. I want to apologize for not accepting them the first time."

"I thought maybe you didn't like cupcakes. Of course, you could have given them to the dog after I left, except they have chocolate in them, and—"

"—chocolate is toxic to dogs," he finished. "See? You're not the only one capable of trivia."

"But that one isn't so trivial."

"Not to a dog owner. No." He shut his tool chest and secured it with a snick. "I heard the microbrewery on the town square sponsors trivia nights. Maybe we could put all that knowledge to work sometime."

You call that noninvolvement?

Maybe she'd refuse and—

"They do, but it's on Tuesdays."

She moved past him and he caught the scent of grapefruit. "You don't like Tuesdays?"

She pulled a plastic container and cover out of a cupboard. "It's a school night."

Ah, yes. Teddy. She was responsible for her brother. And he was steering clear of that sort of commitment. "Summer's coming."

"You're right—it is. That will give me time to brush up." She arranged cupcakes in the container and put the cover on with a *snap* sound. "I'm weak when it comes to sports knowledge, though."

"That's where I come in," he said and accepted the cupcakes, setting them on top of the cardboard box. "I'll be the strong one when it comes to those categories."

Do you even know what noninvolvement means?

Once in his own kitchen, Gabe set Addie's cupcakes on the counter and took off the cover to grab one. They smelled delicious. Thank goodness she'd renewed her offer.

Radar stood at his feet and watched, unblinking, while he peeled off the paper surrounding the cake part. The dog crowded closer and pressed against Gabe's leg as if to remind him of his presence.

"Sorry, bud, but these are for me. You can't have chocolate in any form whatsoever." He walked across the small kitchen and ran the flat of his hand over the motion-activated cover on the trash can, tossed the paper in and waited for it to close. His life would get more complicated if that dog ever figured out how to get the lid to open. A feat that wouldn't surprise him. Radar was uncannily smart—he'd had to be to survive life on the streets in Kabul—but he was still a dog and not above rooting through the trash.

Just like no matter how much he warned himself about his appealing neighbor, he hadn't been able to stop his reaction to seeing her lacy bra.

And now he had to go buy supplies to wash his Jeep with her brother. But the kid wasn't so bad, and it was obvious he was thirsty for some male bonding. His father had always made time for him. Even when he'd probably been dead tired from working two low-paying jobs.

Although he hadn't gotten the chance, he liked to think he'd have been as good a father to his own son as his pa had been to him. He sighed and pulled open the refrigerator. It had been easy to block out thoughts of the past while trying to stay alive in some war-torn hellhole.

He tried to imagine what his life would've been like if his son had lived, if he and Tracy had stayed together, if he hadn't joined the marines. Would they have been on a street like this, tossing the ball around in the front yard? Would he have been able to provide for his family?

When the economy had taken a downturn and construction work dried up, they'd moved in with his pa. He'd already been contemplating the military when Tracy lost the baby at almost eight months.

That plan had then gotten shelved, at least temporarily.

He shook his head. What was he doing standing here with the refrigerator door open?

Grabbing a longneck, he ambled into the living room with Radar on his heels. He sank onto the couch, put his socked feet on the coffee table and grabbed the remote for the new television he'd splurged on. Maybe some baseball in high-def would help occupy his thoughts, keep him from playing what-if.

Addie deposited items on the polished wood counter of Loon Lake General Store. She'd run in to grab a couple of things while Teddy was at his Scout meeting.

"I hear Gabe Bishop moved into the other side of your duplex," Tavie Whatley, the seventysomething owner of the store, commented as she rang up the items.

"Yes, he did." Last thing she needed was another person trying to matchmake her with Gabe. And the elderly shopkeeper was anything but subtle. The woman had her hand on the pulse of practically everything in town. She was the person you called when you wanted results. Many referred to the woman as a benevolent dictator. Her heart was in the right place, but her methods could be a bit heavy-handed.

"Is it true he's got a military-type dog with him? I hear tell he dragged that dog with him all the way from Afghanistan."

"Yeah, the dog is from Afghanistan," Addie answered cautiously, wondering where this was heading. She glanced at her watch. Pic-N-Save was farther away from the church where the Scouts were meeting, but it may have been faster after all. The Pic-N-Save cashiers were friendly, but most didn't give her the third degree.

"Since he's your new neighbor and everything, I was thinking we should get him to help get Pets for Vets off the ground."

Addie bit her lip. Pets for Vets was the most ambitious project ever discussed at Coffee & Conversation. Not only would the program be expensive, but it would require more expertise than anyone who attended the meetings had. The purpose would have been to provide pets to veterans wanting companionship and the comfort animals could provide. "I didn't realize we were going ahead with that. I thought we'd decided it might be more than our little group could handle."

"*Harrumph.* Now that Gabe is back and has his own dog, it's the perfect time to revive this." Tavie patted her sprayed helmet of gray hair.

"I get that a program like that would be a great help to some of our local veterans, but I only mentioned it in passing because of that television segment. I thought I was making conversation about a charity that provided comfort animals to veterans. I certainly wasn't championing doing anything like that with our little group." She needed to learn to keep her big mouth shut. She should know by now that nothing was ever just conversation if it was said within earshot of Tavie.

"But it's a perfect idea. Give yourself some credit, Addie." She bagged up the purchases.

"I really can't take credit for this." She held up her hand. Really and truly she couldn't. She wouldn't.

"Sure you can." She reached out, her gnarled fingers covering Addie's. "Tell Gabe to come to the next community meeting and we'll take it from there."

She picked up her bags but paused at the door. "Well, I—"

"Sorry to rush you, sweetie, but I gotta be closing up. Ogle will be wanting his supper." Tavie came from behind the counter and opened the door, making the old-fashioned bell jingle merrily.

Five minutes later, Addie found herself banished and standing in the parking lot as the older woman shut off the lights inside the store. How exactly had she gotten railroaded into asking—excuse me, *telling*—Gabe to come to the community meeting at the library?

She swore as she opened her car door. "And I'm not putting any money in the stupid swear jar. So there," she told the universe as she got behind the wheel and started the engine.

Yeah, who was she kidding? She'd meant what she said about using the honor system.

She made a mental note to check up on that charity. Maybe she could contact them and find out more about it.

Her new neighbor hadn't said Radar was a trained comfort canine, but she couldn't help noticing that the dog appeared to have sensed his master's moods and reacted. She may not have thought about it at the time—too busy being frightened of the dog—but she'd observed the animal leaning against Gabe's leg. Was that some sort of signal?

She pulled into the parking lot of the historic white church just as the kids were coming out of the side door that led to the meeting area in the basement. Teddy came out with one of the leaders and she rolled down the window and waved. Her brother spotted her and ran to the car.

"What's in the bag?" she asked after he'd climbed onto the booster seat. She didn't pull out of the parking spot until she heard the click of the seat belt.

"A stupid block of wood."

Oh dear, sounded like Scouts hadn't gone well. Thinking that he could make friends and build some normal childhood memories, she'd encouraged him to join. This wasn't the first time she'd worried about a decision. Nowadays, she questioned her choices a lot.

"They must've given you a block of wood for a reason." She glanced in the rearview mirror. Teddy stared out the window, arms crossed. And, oh my God, he looked like he might start crying. *Addie, what have you done?*

"They said it's to make a miniature race car for the Pinewood Derby. But it's just a stupid block of wood. I asked if I could make one outta LEGO bricks 'cause I know how to do that, but Joey's dad said no. Then Joey tol' Brandon that I didn't have a mom or dad...just a sister."

She had trouble dragging air into her tight chest. Why did kids have to be so cruel? "Where was Mr. Johnson when Joey said this?"

"He was on the other side of the room, helping Timmy tie a square knot."

Yeah, a kid like Joey knew enough not to say mean stuff in front of adults. "Who's Brandon?"

"A new kid. Now he probably thinks there's something wrong with me," he said and sniffed.

"There's nothing wrong with you. Don't ever think that. There's lots of kids who don't have parents to live with."

"None at my school."

Her throat began to clog and she tightened her grip on the steering wheel. What was she supposed to say? She had a feeling telling him he was special was the wrong thing.

In the end, she simply told him she was sorry.

What else could she say? She'd talk with the family counselor again for some advice. The fact she had lots of people in her life she could turn to didn't alleviate the sadness of not having parents to turn to for advice.

She pulled onto their street and slowed as they got near their home. "Maybe I could help you make a pinewood racer."

"Do you know how?" His question sounded like an accusation.

"Not yet. We'll look it up. I'm sure we can find a video to show us how—"

"Look, Addie, look. Mr. Gabe and Radar are outside in the yard. Do you see them?"

"Yes, sweetie, I see them."

She pulled into the driveway on her side of the building with a sigh of relief. At least Teddy was temporarily distracted from his problems. For the moment, anyway.

He undid his seat belt. "Hurry, Addie, hurry. Before they go back inside."

She gathered up her bags and exited to let him out. Teddy was off like a shot as soon as she opened his door.

Radar looked to Gabe, who nodded. Evidently that was all the signal he needed, because Radar ran to Teddy, and they greeted one another with barks and giggles.

"You found it," Teddy shouted, holding up a tennis ball.

Gabe motioned to the dog. "He did."

"Did he look both ways before crossing the street?" Teddy asked as he picked up the ball.

Gabe nodded. "We did."

"You remember that yourself next time," she cautioned and shook her head. "Sometimes I think it goes in one ear and out the other."

"I'm sure my pa thought that about me at his age." Gabe chuckled. Sobering, he shook his head. "And a decade later, for sure."

Was he referring to his early marriage and divorce? She wanted to ask, but there wasn't any way she could dress up pure curiosity as concern.

He pointed to her bags. "Do you need some help with those?"

"No, there's nothing that can't keep." She set them on the stoop.

"Look, Addie, look. We're playing ball," Teddy called and threw the ball for the dog.

"I see that." She lowered herself to the top step and heaved out a sigh. "One of these days, I'm going to change my name and not tell anyone what the new one is."

Gabe threw his head back and let out a brawny burst of laughter before sitting next to her. "You're very good with him."

She pulled her knees up and rested her arms

across them. "You wouldn't be saying that if you'd been with us on the drive over here."

"Want to talk about it?"

"Some of the kids were making fun because he lives with his sister."

"Do you have permanent custody of him or something?"

Normally she wouldn't be discussing this with a virtual stranger, but there was something about sitting on the steps in the fading light of an unseasonably warm spring night. "You heard him tell Radar that his—I should say *our*—mom was sick. She's been in rehab. Not for the first time. Which is why I've filed for permanent custody. We're waiting for the hearing in family court."

He blew his breath noisily between his lips. "That's a lot to take on at your age."

"I'm older than I look." She fisted her hand. Maybe telling him wasn't such a good idea.

He reached over and took her curled hand in his. "I didn't mean it as an insult. You're what? Twenty-one? Most people your age are trying to figure out what they want to be when they grow up."

"I'm almost twenty-three," she said but found it hard to concentrate with her hand in his warm, calloused one. She fought the urge to lean against him.

"You're using the prefix *almost* and adding time to your age."

"Maybe I ought to start counting my age in dog

years. I'd be what? One hundred and fifty-four." She rubbed her temple. "No. Wait. That would make me three and a half."

He barked out a sharp laugh. "Whoa. That's way too young."

"Yeah, well, I guess everyone seems young when you're ancient," she shot back without any real rancor. "Exactly how old are *you*?"

"Almost thirty-one," he said with a cheeky grin.

"See? Ancient," she said, but she wasn't sure he'd even heard her. His attention seemed to be on her lips.

He leaned closer, and instead of pulling back, she moved toward him, her hand still in his. Saliva flooded her mouth at the thought that he might kiss her. Would he? How would those full lips feel on hers? Would the stubble on his face be soft or—?

"Addie? Hey, Addie."

She jumped back at the sound of Teddy's voice. Folding her hands, she rested them on her lap where they couldn't get her into any trouble. She swallowed, twice. "What is it, Teddy?"

"Can I ask Mr. Gabe if he knows how to make pinewood racers?"

"Do you want him to ask?" she said out of the side of her mouth.

"What are they?" he whispered back.

"I haven't had a chance to look up to see how it's

done, but it's a small block of wood that gets turned into a race car."

"Wood? I can probably work with that."

She turned toward Teddy. "You may ask."

Addie yawned after tucking Teddy in bed and switching off his light.

After the Scout meeting, Teddy had been sullen, but Gabe had quickly changed that when he'd used his phone to look up pinewood racers. He showed Teddy pictures of finished miniature cars and they discussed which ones appealed to him.

What a difference that thirty minutes in Gabe's company had made. By the time they'd come into the house, Teddy had been excited for the derby.

Time had nothing to do with the difference in Teddy's attitude.

"Give credit where credit is due. It was Gabe and Radar," she reminded herself as she pulled Teddy's door shut.

She hoped she wasn't making a mistake getting involved. And not just for Teddy's sake. He wasn't the only one whose heart could be broken.

Chapter Six

The next morning, after a brief stop at the local vet, Addie drove out to Brody Wilson's farm. Her passenger, safely secured in a cat carrier, was vocalizing her displeasure at her predicament.

"I don't like this any better than you," she told the feral cat and sneezed twice.

So much for the meds she'd taken before this outing. At least her cat allergy was merely annoying, not life-threatening. Despite what might be an allergy to cats, she hadn't minded capturing the scrawny creature when it started hanging around the dumpster in the library parking lot. They'd set out the trap so they could have the cat checked by the local vet. That had been nearly two months ago. The feral feline had been reasonably healthy for a stray. But also very pregnant.

Since the weather had still been cold, Dr. Greer had agreed to board the cat until she gave birth and nursed her kittens. The vet and her staff had made sure the babies were socialized with people so they could be adopted. Unfortunately, the mama cat, which Addie had named Agatha, was too feral to be adopted out.

After reading an online article, Addie felt as though she'd found a solution. The item had talked about such cats being rehomed on farms. When she brought it up at a library meeting, Trudy Canterbury had suggested taking the cat to Brody Wilson. Everyone agreed, saying Brody's farm was virtually an animal sanctuary.

Several people had relayed to her a story about the time Bill Pratt, a local farmer, had brought a calf to Brody in hopes that he'd take her. The mama cow had rejected her offspring, and so it would need to be bottle-fed in order for it to survive. It seemed Bill's young granddaughter was very concerned about the animal's future. Bill had assured the youngster he'd find the calf a good home. Someone had suggested Brody because he'd taken in a pair of abandoned alpacas and nursed them back to health. Bill Pratt told everyone that Brody had assumed responsibility for the young cow in order to impress Mary. Evidently it had worked, because Brody and Mary were now husband and wife. Brody had adopted Mary's young son, Elliott, and was raising the boy as his own.

Addie glanced at the cat carrier and frowned. Tavie had assured her that she'd cleared it with Brody. Maybe she should've called him too, but she'd been running late and didn't want to keep the vet waiting.

"How did I get into this, anyway? Me and my big mouth," she said as her ancient Toyota rumbled over the cattle guard at the end of Brody's driveway.

Everyone had stepped forward with helpful advice and monetary donations, but when it came to taking the cat to Brody, they were all suddenly too busy. They said they thought she was just the right person to take the cat out there, since she'd made the suggestion in the first place. So here she was, with a scrappy cat and a batch of cupcakes to sweeten the deal.

"A spoonful of sugar, right?" she said to Agatha.

Her answer was an angry yowl from the cat carrier.

"Now, don't be like that. Brody has a heated barn, and if the town scuttlebutt is correct, he also has a soft spot for strays. He and Mary both. As a matter of fact, I think all his animals were homeless at one time."

She parked next to the two-story white farmhouse, its shiny red metal roof gleaming in the morning sunshine. A covered porch with wind chimes hung from the rafters ran across the front of the home and wrapped around one side. A cedar play set with a swing sat in the side yard, evidence that this was a family home as well as a business.

Brody and Mary Wilson ran summer camps for children being raised in the foster care system. Although Addie's own time in the system had been short, she, like Teddy, had been forever changed by the experience. So she admired Mary's vision and Brody's hard work transforming his farm and setting up a nonprofit to make Mary's dreams come true. She also admired Brody's relationship with his adopted son. It was plain to see he doted on the little boy, and Elliott worshipped his dad.

"You wait here," she told the cat as she opened the driver's door. The cat hissed in response. "Yeah, I know, silly me. Where else are you going to go?"

Good grief, she was beginning to sound like Gabe with Radar, the way she was chattering away to the cat.

She started up the sidewalk toward the house and glanced over to the barn and the gray Jeep parked there. Was that Gabe's? What was he doing here? Not that it was any of her business where her neighbor spent his time.

As a former Army Delta Force sergeant who'd served in Afghanistan, Brody probably had a lot in common with Gabe. It wouldn't be surprising for them to form a friendship.

"And it's none of your business," she reminded herself. Gabe was her neighbor. The fact he'd been helping, first with her leaking faucet and then with Teddy's race car, didn't give her the right to keep tabs on him.

The wooden screen door opened with a creak and drew her attention away from the Jeep and back to the house. A tall, broad-shouldered man wearing a chambray work shirt and faded denim stepped onto the wide porch. Before the door shut, a young boy with a mop of dark curls and wearing footed dinosaur pajamas scurried out and went to stand next to Brody.

"I'm *El-ee-ot*," the boy said, turning to her and holding up three fingers. "I'm this many olds now."

"Hello, Elliott. Wow, three years old. You know what that means?" She smiled at the winsome little boy, who shook his head. "It means you're old enough to come to story hour at the library. We read stories and do crafts. Doesn't that sound like fun?"

"Mama says no." The boy tilted his chin down and frowned. "Mama says I gotta use the potty first."

Brody ran his hand over the riot of curls in a tender gesture. "But we're working on that, aren't we, big guy?"

"Alice don't got to," Elliott said in a put-upon voice and scowled up at his dad. "How come I gots to?"

Brody sighed as if that was an old argument. "Your sister is just a baby. She doesn't know better and you're a big boy now."

Crossing his arms over his chest, Elliott pouted. "No fair."

Addie rubbed a hand across her mouth to wipe the smile off her face. She loved seeing the two of them together. It told her that there were men in the world who made wonderful dads to children who were not theirs biologically. Could she hope for something like that for Teddy? *And myself*, she thought as her mind went straight to Gabe.

Don't go there, she warned herself. Weaving possibilities around her sexy neighbor could lead to disappointment, and she was responsible for protecting Teddy's tender heart.

She smiled at Elliott. "Well, the crafts and stories will be there whenever you're ready. There's no rush."

She recalled her mother's impatience when Teddy had been potty training. Addie had taken over. That should have been a warning sign of their mother's instability, but she'd ignored it.

Brody patted his son on the shoulder. "It's okay, bud. Go in and get dressed."

"Okay, Daddy." Elliott gave her a heart-melting smile and a wave. "Bye-bye, liberry lady."

"Bye, Elliott."

Brody watched him go back inside. Shaking his

head, he turned back to her. "It will happen eventually, right?"

"The average age for boys to master toilet training is thirty-one months." Brody raised an eyebrow and she continued, "Sorry. It's the librarian in me. All this trivia roiling around in my head. Sometimes it overflows and comes out through my mouth. Yuck, that sounded gross, didn't it?"

"Considering what we were talking about…" Brody took a toothpick out of the pocket on the front of his shirt. He unwrapped it and put it in his mouth. "So, what brings you all the way out here this morning?"

Hadn't Tavie called or was Brody giving her a hard time for the pure enjoyment of it? If so, she could play along. "I'm here to talk about a fantastic employment opportunity."

"What? How did you even hear about it?" He scratched his head. "Anyway, I'm sorry to say you're a couple hours too late. It's been filled."

"What?" Had someone else from the group sneaked out here before her to rehome a feral cat as a barn cat?

He shifted the toothpick from one side of his mouth to the other. "Forgive me for saying this, Addie, but he was more what I was looking for."

Her throat tightened as she glanced over her shoulder at her car. What was she going to do now? The cat was totally feral. No one would adopt her. "Are you sure you couldn't use another one?"

"Another one? I'd love to help you out but…" Brody frowned. "What happened to your job at the library? I would have thought that—"

"Oh no! I think there's been some sort of mis-communication." She exhaled and chuckled. "The job isn't for me. It's for Agatha."

"Agatha?"

"She's been hanging around the library and—"

He held up his hands, palms out. "Hold on. What exactly are we talking about here?"

"The feral mama cat we rescued. I thought Tavie was going to call and explain it to you." Addie huffed out an annoyed breath. "She said she was going to reach out."

"Yeah, it's never good when Tavie calls me." He shrugged sheepishly. "I may not have returned her message yet."

"Great." Her shoulders slumped. "If you didn't talk to her, then that means I've shown up here—out of the blue—trying to dump a stray cat on you."

He moved the toothpick around his mouth. "Pretty much, yeah."

"I'm sorry." What was she going to do? After telling Teddy all this time that they couldn't afford a dog, it wasn't as if she could take the cat back home with her.

"Addie?" He held up his hand. "Just explain what's going on."

"I promise this isn't so bad. We all chipped in and

had Agatha spayed after her kittens were weaned," she said, wanting to make sure he didn't think he was going to be responsible for placing kittens.

Brody pulled another toothpick from his pocket, touched the one in his mouth, grimaced and put the wrapped one back into his pocket. "Exactly how many kittens am I expected to house?"

"Oh no, I'm not asking you to take kittens. They've all been weaned and placed in good homes, so that just leaves the mama. Agatha's recovered from her spaying, but she's totally feral, so placing her with a normal family is out of the question."

He gave her an affronted look. "Are you calling my family—?"

"Absolutely not." Good Lord, talk about messing this up in every way possible.

Note to self: never let anyone volunteer you for anything again.

Maybe she should have asked for Gabe's opinion. After all, he'd gone to Afghanistan and had returned with a dog. She didn't know the specifics, but even with her fear, she could see that Radar was devoted to Gabe and he to the canine.

What was she thinking? Yes, he'd helped out with Teddy last night, but she couldn't start running to Gabe every time she had a problem, expecting him to help solve it.

Brody quirked an eyebrow. "So, what are you asking me to do?"

She needed to quit mooning over Gabe and get this back on track. "Well, considering you have a nice barn and outbuildings, we were hoping you could use a good mouser. We thought she'd make a great farm cat. She could live in the barn and be out of the elements in winter and be fed regular meals. We also chipped in and bought cat food so—"

"Okay. Okay. You've sold me. We were meant for one another. Any more convincing, and I'll need waders." He rolled the toothpick in his mouth and narrowed his eyes. "What I want to know is, who is this *we* you keep talking about?"

"Mostly the attendees of the Coffee & Conversation meetings at the library and a few generous patrons who heard about what we were doing." A donation box at a few key locations in town hadn't hurt either.

"I see." He lowered his eyebrows at her. "Miss a few meetings, and suddenly there's a Brody'll-do-it list, is that how it works? I'm not the only one in Loon Lake with a barn. What about Bill Pratt of Hilltop Farm? Why couldn't he—?"

"He already has several barn cats," she said and swallowed her laugh. Bill had been gleeful while relaying the story of the calf to her.

"Is that what he told you?" He pointed the toothpick at her. "Let me guess. He was at the meeting."

She nodded and he shoved the toothpick back into his mouth.

"He was, and you weren't there to object when your name came up." Relief unfurled the knot in her stomach. Brody might grumble and complain, but it went against his nature not to help. Just like Gabe jumping in to help Teddy turn his block of wood into a race car.

He tsk-tsked. "I guess I assumed you'd have my back, Addie."

"What can I say? I'm only one person."

"No wonder your meetings are so popular," he said but moved off the steps. "People go to protect themselves."

"That, and Natalie's baked goods." Her red velvet cupcakes were good, but the disappointment in the room was palpable anytime attendees discovered Natalie—and, more important, her treats—wasn't going to be at the meeting. The red velvet cupcakes—the ones she'd risked missing Teddy at the bus stop for—couldn't hold up against anything her friend chose to bake.

"Yeah, as soon as poor Des tasted those, he was well and truly captured. Poor guy was— What?" he asked, all innocence when she shot him a glare.

"He wasn't captured. That's a terrible thing to say," she told him but ruined her scolding by laughing. "They fell in love. Just like you and Mary."

"Not the same at all." He shook his head. "I can't imagine what Natalie sees in a grump like Des. As for me, Mary and Elliott couldn't resist my charming personality."

He held up a finger when she opened her mouth to respond. "Ah, now, Addie, don't forget I'm the one you're asking to do a favor."

"Got it. Charming personality." She smothered another laugh.

They might be teasing and joking around, but the forever families both Des and Brody had created gave her hope that someday she might find that. Once again, Gabe came into her mind's eye and she shoved him away. She and Teddy were a package deal.

"Speaking of Des, why didn't you take the cat to him? He has a barn."

"True, but as you said yourself, he's such a grump. Whereas *you*, with your charming personality..."

"I'm going to have a moat and a drawbridge installed at the end of that driveway," he muttered but followed her to her car.

She used her key fob to unlock the trunk.

His mouth dropped open. "You brought the cat in your trunk?"

She rolled her eyes at him. "The cat is in a carrier on the front seat. The food is in the trunk. You can carry the food and I'll get Agatha."

With a grunt, he removed the humongous bag of dry kibble and the carton of canned food from the trunk. "Remind me again—what's wrong with this cat? Other than its name."

She opened the passenger door and grabbed the carrier. "There's nothing wrong with her or her name. She was never socialized, so she's skittish around people."

"Only because she hasn't met my Mary yet. She'll have that cat eating out of her hand in no time."

"And here I thought you were the charming one in the family." She raised an eyebrow at him.

"Thin ice, Addie, thin ice." He shifted his bundle and thrust his chin at her, but ruined the gesture with a huffed-out laugh. "If this cat's not into people, how do you know she'll stay long enough to eat all this food?"

"Well, if your charismatic personality doesn't win her over, I'm sure a dry barn on rainy days or long winter nights and a consistent food source might. That should go a long way to convincing her to make this her new home." Maybe she should try again to convince Teddy to settle for a cat. She sneezed. She'd put up with what appeared to be an allergy if it would make Teddy happy. Except the last time she'd mentioned it, he'd said he'd be happy with a cat if he also had a dog.

"Tell me she's not going to be a threat to Serenity."

"What?" She set the carrier down while she sneezed several more times.

"Mary's crow, Serenity."

"And you're giving *me* grief over a name?"

Brody grunted. "Mary named it."

Chuckling, she picked up the carrier and resumed following Brody toward the barn. "That's right—I forgot she rescued one and earned its undying gratitude. Crows have the intelligence of a seven-year-old, so they're probably smarter than the cat. I don't see it as a problem." *Let's hope.* "Hear that, Agatha. No messing with the crow."

At the barn, Brody set the bag and box on the ground to roll open one of the giant double doors, releasing the scent of hay, horses and sawdust. Addie blinked to adjust her eyesight from the bright sunshine to the dim interior. Hooks holding things like bridles, halters, shovels, a pitchfork and numerous tools lined much of the rough wood walls. Although she hadn't had a lot of experience in barns, she figured this one was scrupulously clean.

Brody picked up the cat food and hefted his burden higher. He pointed toward a partitioned room with an open door in one corner of the vast barn. "Let's get everything set up in the office. I'll get a metal trash can to keep the food safe from critters."

"I hadn't thought of that," she confessed.

"Well, if Agatha—we may have to revisit that name—does her job, then there shouldn't be any critters to get into the feed."

"I guess you have a point." At least he was being good-natured about her essentially showing up and dumping a cat on him. She didn't know the full story of Gabe and Radar, but it couldn't have been easy getting the dog to this country. Another admirable quality. As if she didn't already have enough to admire about him.

"And there's nothing wrong with Agatha's name," she felt compelled to add.

"Uh-huh. I have a wooden box we can put an old blanket in to make a bed," he said as he led her into the office and placed the bag just inside.

He closed the door with his foot and set the canned food on a large metal desk cluttered with paperwork. "I figured we could put out some food and leave her in here for a bit so she knows this is where it is."

"Good idea. I'd hate for her to bolt before she gets to know the place." Addie set the cat carrier on the floor.

Brody opened a desk drawer and pulled out a ceramic ashtray. "Don't worry. It's clean. Been clean for a few years now."

He dumped the contents of one of the cans into the makeshift dish and set it down. "I'll open the cage and let her come out when she's ready."

"She'll probably wait for us to leave." She unzipped the opening to the carrier and stepped back, but the cat, for all her vocal complaints, huddled in the corner.

Yeah, she could relate. After her experiences, she found trusting people difficult—especially when it came to Teddy. She saw her friends together, Brody with Mary and Natalie with Des, and yearned for a close, loving relationship of her own. Of course, that would mean learning to trust again. If she couldn't open up, she might end up in a solitary life like Agatha.

"So, you can call me with any questions or if you have any problems. She's been to the vet recently, so she's up to date on that. If you have any issues with, um, with—"

"We can afford to take care of it." His brow pulled into an affronted frown. "If that's what you were trying to say."

You and your big mouth. First, she insulted Gabe and let him know the local gossip had been about him, something she deeply regretted. She hadn't meant to hurt or insult anyone. "Sorry. I only meant—"

He held up a hand. "It's okay. Getting the camps up and running wasn't easy, but even with the expansion, we're on solid footing with them now. Mary makes sure to keep us afloat. She leaves no stone unturned when it comes to finding grant opportunities."

"That's right. You do some weeks for kids with cancer."

"Yeah. Liam and Ellie McBride help out a lot with that." They left the office and he started to shut the door behind them but paused and looked to her for confirmation.

She nodded. "Keep it closed for a short while."

"Gotcha. She needs to get her bearings." He eyed the surrounding area. "I could put in a cat door. That might help."

Addie smiled. No wonder everyone had suggested bringing the cat here. Did Gabe have a soft underbelly like Brody? Was that how he'd ended up rescuing Radar and doing what was necessary to bring him to this country? He'd certainly been offended on the dog's behalf when she'd suggested that Teddy could have been bitten.

"You can wipe that Cheshire-cat grin off your face right now, Addie Miller. This is not an animal sanctuary and I am not a pushover."

Still grinning, she made an X over her heart. "The thought never crossed my mind."

He scowled, but his eyes held more amusement than annoyance. "So, when is the next meeting?"

"Meeting? I— Oh, you mean at the library. Next Tuesday at noon."

"I guess I'd better make a note of that."

She shrugged. "You could always send Mary."

"Ha! She'd have me signed up for everything."

"And you wouldn't be able to say no to her."

He heaved an exasperated sigh, but his face turned all soft. "I haven't figured out a way yet."

As they stepped from the barn, a dog bounded

around the corner in a blur. Heart pounding and adrenaline coursing through her veins, Addie darted behind Brody so he was between her and the animal. She went rigid with fear.

"Halt," came a sharp order from somewhere on the other side of the building, and the dog immediately obeyed and went down on all fours.

Breathe, damn it, breathe.

Brody frowned and glanced over his shoulder at her. "Relax. That's just Radar. He won't hurt you."

It took a moment for the information to implant itself in her brain. Yes, it was Radar.

She relaxed slightly when she recognized both dog and owner's voice. She might not have conquered her fear of dogs, but instinct told her Radar wouldn't hurt her.

"Gabe is here?" Which was a stupid question because not only had she recognized his Jeep earlier, but she'd just heard his voice.

Her breathing still shallow and her legs wobbly, she fought to regain control over her apprehension.

Despite their short acquaintance, she found the thought that Gabe was nearby comforting.

Chapter Seven

Gabe swore as he slammed the cover on the clip-board he'd been using to make notes in the expanded bunkhouse. Radar surely couldn't get into any trouble on Brody's farm, but Gabe figured he'd better check to see what had attracted the dog's attention.

Radar had been entertaining himself chewing on a Kong chew bone while Gabe worked. The dog's ears had perked up, and he'd dropped the toy, dashing off.

He'd yelled for the dog to stop but couldn't be sure Radar would obey the command. If he wasn't going to behave, bringing him along in the future would be out of the question. This morning all he'd been doing was working up an estimate. Brody had wanted to hire him for some finish work on the bunkhouse expansion. He wasn't sure if working construction was what he wanted long-term, but for now, it would get him out of the house. Maybe even prevent all those extreme thoughts of his tempting neighbor.

As he came around the side of the barn, he understood Radar's enthusiasm. At least the dog had obeyed his command and was lying with his belly on the ground. But his tail was brushing the dirt, kicking up little dust plumes.

"Sit," he said, and the dog sat up, but he didn't release him. Addie's fear was plain, despite what he assumed were attempts to conceal it.

He vowed then and there to help her overcome her fear. If she let him. Some instinct told him she didn't trust easily, but he'd give it his best shot.

Because it was the right thing to do and not because he couldn't stop thinking about those dimples when she graced him with a genuine smile. Or how much he wanted to kiss those freckles.

Yeah, he was a real humanitarian.

"He must've heard your voice and took off. Probably hoping Teddy was with you."

She shook her head. "He's in school. I was just dropping off a homeless cat."

"Dropping off a homeless cat?"

"It had been hanging around the library, and I was worried about it. Unfortunately, it's feral, so it needed a special placement. Brody has agreed to let it stay in his barn. It will make a good mouser. I couldn't stand the thought of it languishing in a shelter or—" she shivered "—having to be put down. At least this way I'll know it's safe, warm and fed."

"So, you *do* like animals…just not dogs." He'd suspected that fear was the motivation for her reactions to Radar.

Her head snapped up. "I never said I didn't like dogs."

"So, it's not dogs in general…just mine," Gabe said, and Radar whined as if in agreement.

"Now you're making assumptions. Both of you," she said, straightening her shoulders.

He scowled. The fact she was including Radar when she spoke made his stupid heart pump a bit faster. Just like when she'd thanked him for preventing Teddy from running into the street.

"Sorry, guys. As fascinating as this is—" Brody cupped a hand around his ear "—I hear my Mary calling me."

"Sorry. I—"

"I didn't mean to—"

They looked at Brody as if he'd appeared out of thin air.

Removing the toothpick from his mouth, Brody guffawed and shook his head. "Just what I thought. Love to stay and referee—I mean, *chat*—with you two kids, but duty calls."

Gabe narrowed his eyes and glowered, not appreciating Brody's smug expression. As if he saw something Gabe couldn't. Or didn't want to. Working construction and getting involved with a woman he had no business getting involved with. Talk about déjà vu.

All the guys had been enamored with Tracy back in high school, and he, the boy from the wrong side of the tracks, had won her attention. Dating Tracy had fed his ego.

And we know where allowing the little brain to think for the big brain ends up.

He tensed when Addie gave Brody a hug. Radar whined and gave him an accusing look, as if telling Gabe it was his fault she was hugging someone other than him. He included the dog in his sour thoughts.

Yeah, because he'd been thinking the same thing. He wanted her hugging him, not another man. Was that his ego talking again?

"Thanks so much for taking the cat," she said and pulled away from Brody.

"Yeah, yeah. I'm a regular saint," Brody replied and turned to Gabe. "I'm sure you can testify to that."

Gabe cupped his ear. "Is that Mary I hear?"

Brody made a face. "Point taken. Got what you needed?"

Gabe nodded. "I'll get some figures written up and give you a call."

Brody nodded and turned his attention to Addie. "And don't worry. I'll check on your cat in a bit."

She raised her brow. "*My* cat?"

Brody harrumphed. "Agatha, you say? Sounds like a maiden aunt."

"Or the greatest mystery writer that ever lived," Gabe said.

Her eyes widened and he did his best not to preen when she rewarded him with a dimpled smile. Score one for those hours spent in his bunk reading mysteries to escape from his reality. Both during his time in school and again in Afghanistan.

"And that's my cue to leave. Play nice, you two." Chuckling, Brody headed toward the house with a backward wave. The side door to the farmhouse opened and closed, but Gabe only had eyes for the woman in front of him.

She motioned with her hand in the direction of her car. "Well…I guess I'd better get going too."

He fought the urge to reach out and physically stop her from leaving. "I don't want to keep you if you're on your way to work."

"I'm not. I had some personal time coming, so I took today off. I wasn't sure how long this would take me." She took a step toward her car.

Radar looked up at him and whined.

Say something. He cleared his throat. "I haven't been to Aunt Polly's since returning home. Are the pancakes still as good?"

She gave him a quizzical glance. Which he totally got because he wasn't sure where this was going. Served him right for giving voice to the outlandish thoughts in his head when she was near. He glared at the poor dog as if this was all his fault.

"I don't know what they were like before you left, so I may not be the best judge," she said. "But Teddy and I love them. My favorite are the buckwheat ones with warm maple syrup."

His gaze zeroed in when she licked her lips, and he swallowed a groan. "I was always partial to gingerbread with whipped cream."

"Teddy always wants whipped cream on his. He doesn't like maple syrup."

Gabe clutched his chest. "What? That's practically sacrilegious in these parts."

"Tell me about it. We've been accused of being flatlanders because of it," she said, using Vermonters' term for non-natives.

He laughed along with her. He quite liked that laugh, especially if he was the one making her do it.

He'd been six years old when his mom died, but he recalled Pa saying over the years how much he missed her laugh. "Your ma would've laughed at that," Pa would say with a sad smile. He hadn't really appreciated his father's sentiment…until now. It wasn't simply the sound of Addie's chuckle but the way her blue eyes sparkled and the way her cheeks dimpled.

This wasn't simple ego. He had a deep longing to

connect with Addie the way he imagined his father had with his mother. If his mom had lived, would he find it easier to connect with a woman now?

Radar pressed his cold wet nose against Gabe's hand, jerking him out of his head. She had taken a few steps toward her car.

"Um…" he began.

She stopped and glanced back with an air of expectation. Yeah, what was he doing?

He cleared his throat. "Would you like to go for pancakes? Well, I mean, you don't have to have pancakes. I just thought you, uh, might like to go to Aunt Polly's."

Radar looked up at him. *Okay, dog, you're right.* That was a bit pitiful, but it had been a while since he'd asked a pretty girl on a date. Date? No, this wasn't a date…exactly. More like two neighbors going for coffee. It wasn't even noon, for crying out loud.

She studied him for a few seconds. He wasn't holding his breath. Nope. Not at all.

"Okay. I'd like that." She gave a decisive nod. Glancing at her car, she said, "I'll meet you there?"

His breath whooshed out. "Sounds good."

See, it's not a date. It wasn't even noon and they were going in separate cars. The fact it wouldn't make sense to leave either vehicle here at Brody's farm was beside the point.

"Retrieve your bone," he said to Radar and pointed in the direction they'd come.

Radar tore off that way, his tail wagging wildly. Gabe had barely gotten the passenger door open when the dog came loping back, jumped in and dropped his bone on the passenger seat. He settled himself next to the black rubber chew. Inching forward, he fogged the windshield with his whining and panting as Addie drove her Toyota down the driveway.

Gabe slipped into the driver's side and started the car. Radar divided his attention between watching Addie's Corolla and giving Gabe what were clearly accusing looks.

"Cut me some slack, will ya? I know it wasn't my smoothest delivery, but she agreed to meet me at Aunt Polly's. So it's all good."

He couldn't be sure, but the dog seemed to understand, because he finally settled back to enjoy the ride. Gabe also enjoyed it. He found the countryside with its rolling hills and grazing cattle soothing after having been in dusty brown, war-torn areas for so long. Once in town, he admired the tidy, brick-fronted businesses and their bright awnings. Several buildings, including the church, dated back to the Revolutionary War, he knew.

Did the town still go all out decorating for Christmas and Independence Day? Main Street in Christmases past had always been awash with lights and wreaths with giant bows. His memories of Christmas were surprisingly pleasant. His pa had done his best to see that Gabe had received at least one frivolous gift, or, as he'd called it, a not-socks gift. Flags and bunting replaced the wreaths on the Fourth of July. His father had taken him to see the town's fireworks display. He recalled holding tight to Pa's hand, trying not to flinch at the loud explosions and failing. If his son had survived, would they have done the same? He liked to think he'd have held his son's hand in reassurance too.

He slowed as soon as he spotted Addie waiting at the entrance to the popular café.

"I told you she'd be here," he said to the dog as he pulled into a diagonal parking spot in front of the town's popular eatery.

"Sorry to disappoint you, but you'll have to wait outside."

The dog made his life-isn't-fair whine and hung his head.

Gabe jumped out of his Jeep and fed the parking meter before he looped the leash handle over the meter. Reaching back into the vehicle, he pulled out the new gadget he'd bought online. It was a portable water bottle with attached dish. He set it down in front of Radar and promised to sit by the window to keep an eye on him just in case. Although, he wasn't overly worried because this was Loon Lake and not many people would want to mess with a dog of Radar's size.

Yeah, he did a good imitation of a guard dog, but the pup was a big softy.

Radar had no choice in his appearance, but Gabe had, by choice, taken on a disguise. First as a trouble-making teen and later as a badass marine.

Yeah, they were two of a kind.

Addie couldn't help the little shiver of anticipation as Gabe tended to Radar. When was the last time she'd had a real honest-to-goodness date?

Slow down, girl. This isn't exactly a date.

It might not be, but she'd worn a silly smile on her face the entire drive to town from Brody's place. When Gabe had first mentioned Aunt Polly's, her pulse had increased and her head had filled with will-he-or-won't-he? thoughts. You'd think she was some teenager wondering if the cute boy in class would ask her to the prom.

Her appreciation of his qualities had increased when he'd picked up on her naming of the cat, and he hadn't laughed. Or at least not so anyone would notice.

And when he had asked if she wanted to go for pancakes, she'd had to take a moment to compose herself. She hadn't wanted to embarrass herself by appearing too eager.

Whatever you do, don't refer to this as a date, she cautioned herself as he approached. "Radar looks so disappointed at not being able to join us for—" *not a date, Addie!* "—uh, for pancakes."

Gabe glanced back at the Jeep. "I guess he'll be okay. I promised to bring him a treat if he behaved."

"We can sit by the window," she said, and her insides melted at the way Gabe's hazel eyes softened when he looked at the dog.

This man really had a good heart. And if she wasn't careful, he'd be stealing hers. And maybe the dog too, because he no longer seemed as scary as he had that first day. "Did that satisfy him?" He shrugged and she continued, "Even if he's only of average intelligence, he's capable of learning approximately one hundred and sixty-five words." She groaned inwardly. Why was she quoting trivia again? This might not be a date, but it already had developed all the awkwardness of one.

"What if he's above average? I've never owned a dog before, but I'm pretty sure this one is exceptionally smart," he said and winced. "Of course, I probably sound just like your typical proud pet owner."

"If he's extra-smart, he probably knows two hundred and fifty or so." Of course, she had no idea how much Radar might have picked up or how long Gabe had had him. "What about you?"

His lips twitched. "I guess I'd have to say I'm about average intelligence."

Warmth rushed into her cheeks. "I meant, do you think he understood?"

"Whew." He swiped a hand across his forehead. "For a minute there, I was afraid you were going to make me recite which one hundred and sixty-five words I've learned."

She laughed as he opened the door to the café. She hadn't had much experience with a man teasing her, but she liked it. Sure, her male friends liked to kid, but that was different. This was definitely different. As was her reaction.

Between trying to keep her mother clean and Teddy taken care of, she hadn't dated in high school. However, once on her own in college, she'd intended to explore guys the way most girls had in high school, maybe even shed her innocence. But her college career hadn't lasted long enough to do either.

She passed him as he held the door for her and was hit with a variety of familiar smells emanating from the restaurant. Coffee, cinnamon and vanilla.

Since it was the slow time between breakfast and lunch, the half-dozen stools in front of the long counter held only two customers. The tables in the middle of the dining area were empty, and only a few of the booths along the front were occupied.

A trim gray-haired waitress greeted them with a cheery "good morning." Her hands full with a coffee-pot in one and two plates stacked with pancakes in the other, she inclined her head toward a vacant booth near the windows facing the street. "Have a seat and I'll be over in a jiff."

Although he didn't actually touch her, Addie noticed Gabe raised his hand so it hovered behind her back as they made their way to the booth. He dropped it as she slid onto the bench seat. He sat opposite her and pulled out the plastic-covered menus that nested between the napkin holder and condiment bottles.

She accepted the one he offered and set it on the table in front of her. "I don't know why I'm looking at this. I always end up ordering the same thing."

He nodded. "It's been a while for me, but these items look familiar."

"Did you miss Loon Lake while you were gone?"

He tilted his head from side to side. "Yes and no. I was glad to leave when I joined the marines, but once I decided to muster out, this was where I wanted to come. That probably makes no sense."

"I can certainly understand it. I had never lived here, and yet I was homesick for a place just like Loon Lake. I'd say I was nuts, except the Welsh have a word for it. They call it *hiraeth*."

He gave her a quizzical frown. "What's that?"

"I can't roll my *R*s, so I know I'm not pronouncing it correctly, but it's something like *hye-ree*. Anyway, it's translated as *nostalgia* or *homesickness*, but it can also apply to yearning for a place that never existed or that you've never experienced personally. I found what I'd been longing for when I moved here."

"Sorry for the wait," the waitress said as she set two ruby-red, pebbled-plastic tumblers filled with water on the table. "Good to see you, Addie, and welcome back to you, young man."

"Nice to see you, Vera," Addie responded. *And thank you for rescuing me before I made a fool of myself.* She mentally kicked herself. What was she thinking, talking about an esoteric concept like *hiraeth* with a hot guy, a former marine at that? Not that he wouldn't understand, but she bet he wasn't as interested as he pretended. "How are you enjoying those cozy mysteries?" she asked the waitress.

"Very much. Thanks for tracking them down for me." Vera leaned closer to Gabe. "I love Addie and our library, but if I want anything racy, I travel over to Burlington or St. Johnsbury, where no one knows me."

"Vera, you know I don't check out books and tell," Addie joked.

"I know, but people here have long memories. I still blush whenever I see Pastor Cook's wife." Vera lowered her voice as she leaned over the table. "She asked what I thought of a certain sexy book when it was hot outside. Ha! Get it? Hot. Sometimes I kill myself. You've read it, haven't you, Addie? I thought—"

"Hey, Vera, quit horning in on Addie's date and get over here and refill my coffee," an elderly man in overalls and a flannel shirt called from across the café.

"Quit your yapping and wait your turn," Vera shot

back. She pulled her pad and pencil from her apron pocket. "Have you decided yet?"

They gave their order and Vera scurried away to give the grumbling customer a piece of her mind along with his coffee refill.

"I'd forgotten how entertaining small-town places like this could be," Gabe said and shook his head at the goings-on.

Should she bring up the fact someone had called this a date? Or should she just ignore it? Like that time he'd almost kissed her. She might be ignoring it, but she certainly hadn't forgotten it. Nor had she stopped imagining it.

Chapter Eight

Addie unwrapped her straw. What the heck—she may as well clear the air. "Just so you know, I don't consider this a date."

His head snapped back. "You don't? What activities do you think constitute a date?"

Buzz. Wrong choice, Addie. "Well…no. I just meant…"

He reached over and captured her flailing hand. "We don't have to label this. How about we just enjoy our pancakes, hmm?"

She exhaled. He was holding her hand, so perhaps she hadn't spoiled whatever this was after all. "Deal."

He gently squeezed her fingers before releasing her. "Tell me how long you've suffered from cyno-phobia."

She inhaled sharply. Why was she surprised? She shouldn't be, because Gabe was an intelligent guy, a battle-tested marine, so he was observant and capable of assessing situations he was in. "You know that I'm afraid of dogs?"

He lifted one shoulder. "I guessed as much, and you've just confirmed it."

She gazed out the window at the activity on Main Street, aware of his intent gaze on her. After getting her thoughts in order, she turned back to him. "I was around Teddy's age when I was bitten. I still have the scars on my stomach and thigh."

His expression grew serious. "What happened?"

"We lived in a duplex—not as nice as ours, but that's beside the point. I was playing by myself in the yard and a neighbor's dog had been roaming freely. I liked dogs and approached it, and it bit me…twice."

He touched his mouth. "Were they serious bites?"

"I was treated in the ER. It was my own fault. I shouldn't have—" She broke off and shook her head. Angry that even after all this time she was ready to parrot Michelle's words. She was no longer seven years old and she was no longer a dutiful daughter. She couldn't be if she was to save Teddy. "No. It wasn't my fault. I was just a kid, but I swear I didn't do anything to the dog to create such a reaction."

He watched her intently. "What made you think it was your fault?"

"I didn't, but my mother made me say it was my fault."

"Why would she do such a thing?"

She inhaled in an attempt to get her riotous emotions under control. "Because she was off getting high when it happened, and when the authorities opened a case file, she didn't want to be charged with neglect. She made me tell the social worker that I had disobeyed her and went over and teased the dog. I—"

"Here you go." The waitress was back with two plates stacked high with pancakes. She set the plates in front of them, frowned, then switched them. "If you need anything else, just holler."

"Thanks," they said in unison.

Vera gave them a sly smile as she wiped her hands down the front of her apron. "Enjoy," she said and left.

Addie buttered her pancakes, then made a small pool of syrup next to the food on the plate. She sliced off a piece and dipped it in the puddle. Sensing his gaze on her, she paused with the fork partway to her mouth and smiled. "That way, I can get a consistent amount of syrup in each bite."

He nodded his head in salute. "Ingenious."

"Or an unquenchable sweet tooth."

"I'll remember that," he said and began to eat.

Her heart tripped up at his words. What did he mean by that? Why would he want to remember that about her? Maybe he was collecting information about her the way she was about him.

"Getting back to what we were discussing, I'm sorry you had such a terrible experience." He took a sip of water. "No wonder you're afraid of dogs."

"She had me convinced it was my fault." Was this why he'd invited her? So they could discuss her fear? "Not only that, but my anger about what happened and the way my mother forced me to accept blame are wrapped up in how I feel about dogs. And I've felt that way about them ever since."

He finished his pancakes and pushed the empty plate aside. "I won't let Radar invade your space, if that will make you feel better."

"No, don't do that, please." She reached across the table and touched his hand as it rested in the empty spot left by his plate. "I hate that I'm afraid. I've wanted to overcome it for a while now. Especially since Teddy loves dogs so much."

"He doesn't know you're afraid?"

She made a face. "Having to confess something like that to my baby brother isn't something I relish. Especially since I'm trying to establish my authority over him."

He flicked his wrist so her hand now rested under his, and his thumb stroked over her knuckles. "You may not want to hear this, but I think it would be best to come clean with him. However, in the meantime, I'd be willing to help you overcome your phobia."

"Do you know what to do?"

"I've been studying up on it."

"You have?" Embarrassment disappeared as quickly as it had appeared, and an unexpected warmth surged through her at the tenderness in his touch. Her heart expanded at the thought that he would go to all that trouble for her. He could have said her fear was her problem and she needed to solve it, which had been her mother's attitude.

Color rose on his cheeks. "A little bit. It's amazing what you find on YouTube."

"Thank you. I'd like that."

"So, what happened with the neighbor's dog and your mother?"

"I never went near the dog or the neighbor ever again. As for my mother, she eventually went into detox. Not that it took. Well, I shouldn't say that. It took for a while. Until it didn't."

"I'm sorry for what you've been through. Both of you," he said, releasing her hand when Vera appeared at their booth with the check.

Addie started to reach for the bill, but he was faster.

"I invited you, so it's my treat," he told her.

"Then let me leave the tip," she said as she dug into her purse for her wallet.

"Deal," he said and went to the register by the door to pay.

As they left, she couldn't help feeling hopeful over Gabe's willingness to assist her. She'd thought he'd laugh at her predicament, but he'd seemed genuinely interested in working with her to overcome her fear.

The entire time Gabe was interacting with the cashier, he was acutely aware of Addie. After setting some bills on the table for the tip, she went and stood by the door to wait. He smiled at the thought of her waiting for him. As if this were a date. Yeah, he'd told himself it wasn't, but as soon as she'd denied it, he'd balked like a rookie pitcher. Date or no, spending time with her was something he enjoyed.

Returning his wallet to his back pocket, he met her at the door. "Would you like to work with Radar after we get home? I'm assuming you might not want Teddy distracting us. He's in school, right?"

"Yes, he is." She smiled and nodded. "That would be great. And, yes, I think it will be easier without an audience."

"So, the backyard, then?" He followed her to her car.

Laughing, she said, "Yeah. I don't need Mrs. O'Malley watching me."

He raised an eyebrow. "The curtain twitcher?"

"She's really sweet, but also very…" Addie pulled on her bottom lip.

A pleasant hum sang through his blood at the sight. What he wouldn't give to be tugging gently on that full lip. He reached past her to open her door for her and cleared his throat. "…observant?"

"Exactly." She slipped into the driver's seat. "See you in a few?"

"Sure thing," he said and closed her door. Who knew such a simple act of courtesy could feel so satisfying?

Flexing his fingers, he watched as she backed out of the parking spot. He had yearned to touch her again before she left, wanted to feel her warm, soft skin under his fingers. Would she be that way all over?

He shook his head in an attempt to shake loose those thoughts. He had no business getting involved with her. She was too young, too caught up in trying to raise her brother. He'd help her with her fear of dogs and then step back.

"Excuse me."

A voice broke into his thoughts. He'd been standing inert in the middle of the sidewalk, and a mother with a baby stroller was trying to get past him.

"Sorry," he mumbled and went toward his car.

Radar, who'd been sitting patiently next to the parking meter, greeted him enthusiastically. Gabe pulled a crumpled napkin from his pocket and un-covered a small piece of bacon.

"Now remember..." Gabe glanced around. "This never happened. Bacon probably isn't any healthier for you than it is for me, but I won't tell if you won't."

Radar practically inhaled the treat.

"Did you even taste it?" Gabe laughed as he opened the driver's door. "And sit on your own side."

The dog whined but jumped in and moved to the passenger seat. After putting the portable watering dish away, Gabe slipped behind the wheel and started the Jeep.

"We're going to help Addie overcome her fear of dogs, so I'm going to need your cooperation." He checked traffic and pulled out of the parking spot. "You'll have to remain calm and submissive. Be on your best behavior. Got that?"

Radar gave a low woof as if in agreement with the plan, and Gabe laughed. He'd taken on the task of getting the pup stateside and assuming owner-ship to honor a fallen friend, but he hadn't hon-estly anticipated how much he'd come to care for him. Gabe had considered Tom one of his closest friends, but Radar was also becoming an integral part of his life.

Just like your new neighbors.

Because he automatically included Teddy. And wasn't that something.

* * *

Addie stopped her pacing long enough to glance out the window for the familiar dark gray Jeep.

"You can do this," she told herself. It would be worth it to spend time with Gabe, right?

The Jeep drove past and she inhaled deeply to calm her nerves. A knock sounded at her front door several minutes later.

She swung it open and gave them both a some-what shaky smile. "C'mon in. We can go through the kitchen to the backyard."

"Radar, heel," he said as he stepped inside. "If you're uncomfortable at any point, be sure to let me know."

"Did you study up on this too?"

His amused gaze met hers. "Why? Do I sound like a YouTube video?"

One of the videos she'd watched about overcoming phobias had talked about replacing bad memories with good. Looking into his eyes, she decided she was halfway there already.

"Maybe I'm just listening like I'm watching one," she said as she led the way through the house and out the back door.

Once outside, Gabe touched her arm. "I'm seri-ous. We'll take this as slow as you want. I want you to be comfortable."

"Thanks. I hate that I have this fear. All my life when I've seen people with their dogs, I've always felt as though I was missing out." She disliked being allergic to cats and afraid of dogs. There were a lot of things in her life that she'd been unable to control, but this fear felt like something she could, should be able to manage.

He had Radar come and sit near her.

"I'm told that the best way is for you to act like a human but to think like a dog," he said.

"How does that work?"

"I'm not totally sure, but it sounded good when the Dog Whisperer said it." He winked.

By the end of an hour, Addie was convinced Radar was the most patient, chill dog she'd ever encountered. *Calm* and *submissive* had been Gabe's words to describe him, and she had to agree.

Although she was quaking inside, she reached over and stroked the velvety fur between Radar's ears.

Of course, she realized that not all dogs were like Radar, but she didn't have plans to interact with every one she met.

As a reward for being so cooperative, Gabe gave the dog his favorite chew toy and released him to go and play with the bone.

"I did it. I was able to pet Radar without suffering a heart attack." As happy as Radar, she threw her arms around Gabe without conscious thought. What was she doing? She felt heat creep up her neck into her face. Even her ears were warm. She would have pulled away, but his arms went around her before she could.

Pulling her close, he fitted her body to his. "I have thought about this ever since Teddy interrupted us."

"Me too," she admitted, his words giving her courage to admit her feelings. She wasn't in this alone. "Why do you think I suggested the backyard instead of in full view of the street?"

"I like the way you think," he said and lowered his head until his lips were inches from hers.

"Like a dog?" she asked.

He laughed, and his breath blew warm on her face. She put her hands on his chest and over his heart until his lips finally brushed across hers. His lips were firm but gentle. She opened her mouth, and his tongue swept in to brush against hers. More, she wanted more.

Not a total innocent, she'd been kissed before, but those had felt more like adolescent fumbling compared to this.

He lifted his mouth and whispered, "I think you're vibrating."

"What?" She pulled herself out of her haze, reluctantly moving away so she could look up at him. "Oh, it's the alarm on my phone. I set it so I wouldn't forget to meet Teddy at the bus stop."

"I guess I was a bit premature with my self-congratulations, huh?"

* * *

She laughed, which was the response Gabe had been going for. It helped lighten the mood, and he loved the sound of it.

He couldn't decide if the interruption of this intimate moment was a good thing or not. After his disastrous first marriage, he'd promised himself he wouldn't let anything like that happen again. Sure, he'd married Tracy after getting her pregnant, but he hadn't stuck around; he had failed her. Worse still, with the clarity of hindsight, he could see that most of his feelings regarding Tracy had involved teen hormones. And the fact that the homecoming queen had shown interest in the kid from the wrong side of the tracks.

In contrast, Addie seemed like the type of woman who would expect him to be a stand-up guy, and he knew his past actions proved he was anything but. He'd just have to explain about his track record and she'd probably run a mile. But he sure liked kissing her. Her kisses were like a drug, one he could become easily addicted to.

Sure, his attraction involved hormones, that was a fact of life, but his feelings toward her went much deeper than that.

He kissed her again, a light peck on the lips, because he couldn't help himself from tasting her one more time. "Would you mind some company on the way to the end of the street?" he asked.

Gabe stepped away from her before he was tempted to deepen the kiss. Tempted? He already was that. And not just tempted to keep on kissing her. Was she wearing another lacy bra today? he wondered.

He shouldn't be doing this at all. Never mind again.

"More exposure therapy?"

She's speaking. Pay attention. "Hmm?"

She grinned as if she'd known his thoughts had been elsewhere. Of course, if she'd known exactly where his thoughts had been, she might not be smiling like that. Or maybe she—

Radar woofed and forced Gabe out of his head. "If you don't want him to come with us to pick up Teddy, I can put him inside."

The dog whined as if he understood he might be left out. He looked to Addie as if he also understood the decision was up to her.

She reached over, gently stroked his head and stepped back, inhaling deeply to calm herself as they'd practiced. "It's okay. He can come."

Gabe put Radar's leash on him, and they walked through the side yard to the front of the house. He couldn't help but notice that, across the street, Mrs. O'Malley's curtain was moving.

"We have an audience," he said in a stage whisper.

Her hands flew to her mouth and he burst out

laughing. "That gesture's not gonna help us look innocent."

She elbowed him but grinned. They fell into a companionable silence for the first part of the walk, but every so often their shoulders would bump. The occasional contact thrilled him, but it went deeper. He felt close to her, a kinship he hadn't felt with anyone since leaving the marines. Like they were linked by common goals and shared objectives. "How did Teddy get the burn scars on his hands and arms?" Acid filled his throat and entered the back of his mouth. Oh man, why in the world had he asked that? Of all subjects to pick, why that? "Forget it. I know it's none of my—"

"It's okay. It's not a big secret or anything. It happened when I was away at college. Michelle—our biological mother—had left him unattended. He pushed a chair over to the sink to sail a toy boat I'd sent him. She'd left a pan of hot water there and he received severe burns when he plunged his hands in to retrieve the toy. The neighbors heard his cries and called the police. They couldn't find Michelle, so of course child services were called in."

Wanting to lend her whatever strength he could, he took her hand. "Child services contacted you?" he prompted.

"No. One of the neighbors had my cell number and called me right after 9-1-1." She sighed. "I just wish she'd contacted me sooner. I would have come home so I could've prevented Teddy from getting burned in the first place. It's all my fault for sending the boat. But he'd kept talking about one when I called, so I found one and mailed it. I figured he'd get a kick out of it."

He winced and swore under his breath. "That doesn't make it your fault."

"I believed her when she said I could trust her. She was done with that stuff for good. Clean and sober. So, I went off to college, left Teddy in her care and—"

"Hold up right there." He stopped and turned to face her. "How old were you?"

"Eighteen."

"You did what millions of people your age do. Going off to college is like a rite of passage for so many high school graduates."

She sighed. "I know, but one of the times I called her, she mentioned how she'd met someone…" She shook her head, her pretty eyes clouded. "I should have come straight home, checked him and the situation out. I knew what happened when she got involved with the wrong guys. I was selfish."

Gabe put his finger across her lips. "She was the mother. You were his sister…practically a kid yourself. Why did you feel it was your job to protect him?"

She shrugged. "It's what I'd always done when I

was home and what I could have done once again, had I been there."

He thought about Tom and that stupid coin toss that had changed everything. They'd argued good-naturedly about whose turn it had been to go into the convenience store. The toss of a coin made Gabe the winner and Tom had to go inside to pay for their drinks. He paid all right, but with his life. Yeah, he knew about guilt, irrational or not.

For the first time since returning home, he had the urge to tell someone about it, but before he could say anything, the school bus arrived.

Just as he had on that first day, Teddy scrambled off the bus and raced over to his sister and Gabe. He once again threw his arms around Radar.

Gabe glanced at Addie, who winced, so he hunkered down so he was eye level with the boy. He touched Teddy's shoulder to be sure he had his attention. "It's good that you and Radar get along so well, but you need to know that not all dogs are as happy to see you as he is."

"Whaddaya mean?"

"I'm just saying that you should find out if the dog is friendly before you reach out."

"But you said Radar wouldn't bite me," Teddy said, and Radar woofed in agreement. "You even tol' that to Addie."

"And that's true, but not all dogs are like Radar,

so make sure you ask the owner if it's okay first."
Gabe lifted his fist. "Deal?"

Teddy did a fist bump. "Deal."

Gabe's heart lurched. Most people might consider
this an inconsequential moment, but to him it was
anything but. He'd never considered himself a sen-
timental guy, but he might have to revisit that opinion since meeting his new neighbors.

Gabe glanced at Addie, who mouthed a thank-
you and seemed to relax a little. He grinned to himself. Yeah, this was a special moment. Small in the
scheme of things, but special to him.

"I'm so glad you're here," Teddy said. "The other
kids on the bus didn't believe me that I live next door
to a hero dog and that he likes me. Now they *have*
to believe me."

"It doesn't matter if the other kids believe it or
not," Addie said. "As long as you know it's true."

Teddy thought about it for a minute, then shrugged.
"But it's better when they know it too."

"You're right. I guess it is." She laughed and reached
out her hand. "Want me to take your backpack for
you?"

He handed it to her. "Mr. Gabe? Can I hold Radar's
leash?"

Gabe glanced at Addie, and after she nodded, he
handed over the leash. He fell into step beside her as
the dog and the boy led the way along the sidewalk.

"Addie, look, I'm walking Radar."

"I see that, sweetie."

Gabe leaned closer. "Thought of a new name for yourself yet?" he asked, referring to her earlier wish for anonymity when Teddy kept using her name.

She thought for a moment, then laughed as if she was recalling her comment too. His stomach did a little somersault.

Another little moment, but monumental in the way it made him feel. Like maybe he hadn't lost everything when he'd lost his son. Maybe second chances were real.

Teddy turned back. "What're you guys laughing at?"

"I'm just happy that you're getting to walk Radar," she told him.

"Mr. Gabe, did you find something for me to help you with today? You said you wouldn't forget. Remember?"

"You're right. I had planned to wash the Jeep today, but it's still kinda chilly outside." The kid looked so dejected, though, that it broke his heart. "I haven't played ball with Radar yet. Maybe you could help with that."

The kid lowered his chin. "Is that *really* like helping you? It doesn't sound much like it."

Busted. He looked to Addie for guidance.

"As much as you love dogs, you should know they require lots of exercise," his sister told him.

"Oh yeah, I forgot."

He waited until Teddy was chattering away to Radar about how they were going to play ball before saying quietly to Addie, "He might have those physical scars, but he seems happy and very well-adjusted."

"Thanks. I still wish I'd been there to prevent the accident." She slowed her steps, letting her brother get even farther ahead with the pup. "What did you mean when you said even when we're there, sometimes we can't prevent the bad stuff from happening?"

"Oh, that." He'd been referring to his being outside the store, only feet away, when Tom was killed. He'd been close enough that he could still smell the cordite, feel the shock waves that had blown him off his feet, taste the soot that had rained down. Did he want to give her an answer? It would mean explaining what had happened, how he'd escaped with his life by winning a stupid coin toss. Just because she'd opened up to him didn't mean he needed to bare his soul. Not yet, anyway—not unless he was going to become a permanent part of her and Teddy's lives. And that wasn't going to happen.

Chapter Nine

Addie mentally kicked herself for spoiling the otherwise touching moment with her probing. His resulting silence told her he didn't want to share. "It's okay. I didn't mean to pry."

"Remember I mentioned my buddy who taught Radar all those commands? He was actually the one who first rescued Radar too. His name was Tom." She nodded and he continued, "We were out on routine patrol through town—"

"In Afghanistan?"

"Yeah. Whenever we were in that part of town, we stopped at this little family-owned store. They had those slushy drink machines. We couldn't get those in camp, so we'd stop, but we couldn't both go in. Someone had to stay with the vehicle. The person going in would pay. This one day, we stopped and argued over whose turn it was to pay."

He winced as if the memory was painful. Inhaling, he continued, "We flipped a coin. Tom lost, so he went into the store. I was waiting outside, standing by the vehicle, when the whole world exploded. I was knocked off my feet by the blast."

Emotion rose in her chest, clogging her throat. Her mother might not have died, but Addie had lost her to the drugs, so she understood that helpless feeling.

"It was a suicide bomber. Everyone inside the store died." He shook his head. "I was how many feet away from Tom? And I couldn't do anything about it."

She wanted to hug him to her, console him, but settled for placing her hand on his arm as they arrived at the duplex. "I'm so sorry. That must've been terrible. Were you badly hurt?"

"I survived."

She squeezed his arm. "Teddy and I are glad you did, and I'm sure Radar is too."

"If I'd lost that coin toss, Radar would be with Tom now."

"And I'd still be afraid of dogs," she reasoned. "You may not think what you did—rescuing Radar like that and bringing him back to America, then starting to help me get over my phobia—is that big of a deal, but believe me, it is, and I—"

"Mr. Gabe?" Teddy interrupted, distracting Addie from her concern over Gabe. "Do you have Radar's ball?"

"Sure. Let me get it," he said and slipped into the house.

"Are you gonna watch me play ball?" Teddy asked.

"Of course. Let me get a couple chairs from the carport." She retrieved two canvas seats. There was just enough room for the both of them on the cement pad in front of the two doors.

Gabe came back out, raising an eyebrow. "Are we the bleachers?"

"Yup."

He tossed the ball to Teddy, who made a running grab for it, but tripped, and the ball went over his head. He started giggling when Radar trotted over and dropped the ball on him.

For the past year, she'd envied her friends for the families they'd formed, but now she was experiencing some of that happiness.

Watching Teddy laughing and playing relieved some of the burden she'd been dragging around like an old suitcase, and she blurted out, "I can't thank you enough for bringing Radar into his life."

He shifted in his seat. "Look, if you're saying that because—because of what I told you before, I wasn't looking for sympathy, reassurance or anything at all when I said it."

"What? No." His reaction shouldn't have surprised her because she knew a lot of veterans wanted to put things behind them. "I'm saying it because I can't help second-guessing everything I do with regards to Teddy."

"Why?"

"I want to keep him safe, but I also want him to have a normal, happy childhood."

"He's a bright, inquisitive boy. I would say you're doing a wonderful job."

"But I'm not his mother…even you said that. What if I'm damaging him?" Okay, so maybe she was having trouble letting go of some of that guilt. After all, she'd had it for a long time. If she'd been able to prevent her mother from relapsing, Teddy's life would be so different now.

"Are you asking me if you're damaging him by keeping him safe, giving him a secure environment to grow up in?"

"Well, if you're going to put it like that…" she said.

Unwilling to explore the feelings he'd churned up, she abruptly changed the subject. "Have you lived your whole life in Loon Lake?"

"Before I joined up, yeah. But I didn't grow up on a street like this." He glanced around the neighborhood. "And it wasn't across town in one of those big Victorians either, if that's what you were wondering."

She hadn't thought that, but he was starting to sound defensive, so she kept silent. She had a feeling her probing earlier had forced a confidence he now regretted. Plus, she didn't want him to stop talking about himself, about his life. Why she wanted to know as much as she could about him was something she was trying not to examine too closely. For all her talk about resisting the town's matchmaking efforts, she realized she was taking an avid interest in All Things Gabe. After that kiss and the time he was spending with Teddy, she could admit to herself her interest in him was swiftly becoming *more* than avid.

"We lived over on the east side on that road that leads to the secluded end of the lake."

"Isn't that the area where someone built that gorgeous log home?" She'd checked out the apartment above the garage after Ellie Harding had moved out, but the place wasn't big enough for both her and Teddy.

He nodded. "Yeah, but it's changed a lot in the past few years. There weren't any houses that impressive back then. The trailer is gone now, but Pa and I lived in a single-wide on an empty lot. No manicured lawns or ornamental bushes, just lots of dirt."

She turned her head toward him and took a moment to admire his profile. God, but he was gorgeous. Not pretty-boy handsome but... Natalie's words popped into her head. He seemed to be lost in the past, staring straight ahead, but not as if he was actually seeing the street or the trees in front of them.

"We moved around a lot, sometimes in the middle of the night when rent was due. Your place may not have been glamorous, but it sure beats a cheap motel," she said, imagining their trailer was a lot better than many of the places she'd lived in when Michelle was using.

"Maybe, but the front yard was nothing but a graveyard for dead lawn mowers and snowblowers. Pa never gave up hope of getting those rusted cast-offs running again. He called them 'precious metals waiting to be mined.'" He shook his head. "Precious, my ass. It was all junk, plain and simple. And if he did manage to get one running, instead of selling it, more often than not, someone had a sob story and he'd end up giving it away, or practically free."

"Sounds like he was caring and compassionate." She laid her hand on his arm.

"Yeah. Too bad his only son was such a disappointment," Gabe said bitterly.

She squeezed his arm. "I find that hard to believe."

"Believe it. His dream was for me to go to college. He didn't get a chance to go himself and really wanted that for me. Make something of myself. He hoped I'd get a baseball scholarship. I might have had a chance…not for the major leagues, though. I wasn't that good."

"What happened?"

"I got the homecoming queen pregnant. Instead of going off to college, I got married and found a job working construction." He huffed out a bitter laugh. "Listen to me. I sound like a Bruce Springsteen song."

"You a Springsteen fan?" He might think of what he did as a cliché, but she knew not all men took responsibility for their actions. She knew two who hadn't. She and Teddy might not share the same biological father, but both men had one thing in common. They'd skipped out. As an eighteen-year-old, Gabe must have been scared by marriage and pending fatherhood, and yet he'd acted with honor. That earned him her respect, even if the marriage hadn't worked out.

He shrugged. "My pa was, so I grew up listening. You?"

"Oh yeah…"

"What? I would have thought he was before your time." He gave her a puzzled glance.

"Remember, I'm one hundred and something in dog years." She couldn't contain her laughter any longer and he joined her.

She was relieved that he wasn't still upset over having confided in her earlier. Her conversation with

Tavie Whatley last night, about inviting Gabe to their community meeting, popped into her mind. And not for the reasons the other woman had suggested. Ogle, Tavie's husband and a Vietnam vet, had managed to get a lot of the local veterans to open up to him. And Gabe could use someone to talk to, someone who understood what he'd gone through, someone who could provide advice on transitioning back to civilian life. They probably said things to Ogle they wouldn't to others. Maybe Gabe could come to terms with what had happened to him in Afghanistan, as well as the circumstances of his childhood and failed marriage.

"Has anyone invited you to our Coffee & Conversation meetings yet?"

He frowned. "Not that I know of."

"Well, now I'm inviting you." She smiled. A spoonful of sugar, right?

"Why?" he asked, giving her a side-eye look.

Maybe she should have bribed him with a real sugar treat. "Why not? Wouldn't you like to get involved in the community? I think it's a great opportunity to get to know people and help out those less fortunate."

"I'm really not interested."

"Oh," she said, because she didn't know what else to say. Until he'd refused, she hadn't realized how much she'd been counting on him agreeing.

She had to ask herself why it meant so much to

her for him to integrate into the community. Had she wanted it for him or for herself? If he was invested in the town, he'd stay, maybe take another chance at creating a family.

Gabe stood up. "You two about done? I hate to break it up, but I have to work up some figures for Brody."

"Of course. I have to see if Teddy has homework before supper." And she wanted to think this over in private.

Even as a child, she'd never been one for fairy tales. So why was she suddenly letting herself act as if her life could be one? Teddy needed to be her top priority, and her dream of having a happy family like her friends needed to stay just that—a fantasy and nothing more. Giving her brother a stable foundation in a safe neighborhood was what she needed to concentrate on, along with finishing her degree and becoming a full-fledged librarian.

Once inside, Gabe called himself all sorts of names. Why had he acted like that? He hated that he'd put that look of hurt on her pretty face. But when she'd talked about people getting together to help the needy, he imagined they'd be looking at him. He had nothing against the good people of Loon Lake, but he could only think how they would be remembering him as one of those less fortunate. His childhood was over.

He had no wish to dredge up all those old memories and the way they made him feel.

Looked like Radar wasn't happy with him either and made his displeasure known by grumbling low in his throat. The dog probably knew he'd acted like a jerk, but after talking about what had happened to Tom, Gabe felt off-kilter. What was it about Addie that made him want to share bits of himself he'd always kept hidden?

Then she'd talked about those community meetings, and it had gotten under his skin.

He went into the kitchen, took two pieces of leftover pizza and a soda from the fridge and threw the food on a plate. After putting the plate in the microwave, he dumped some dry kibble in Radar's bowl and refilled the water dish.

Was she getting supper too? Would she be sitting down to help Teddy with homework? He imagined she would be the type to check over the boy's lessons.

The dog plunked himself down in front of the water dish and noisily lapped up water. The microwave dinged and Gabe took the pizza out. He grabbed the clipboard he'd used at Brody's to take notes and went to the small desk he'd set up in the living room for his laptop.

He'd told Addie he was going to work on figures for Brody, and that was what he'd do. He wasn't going to think about that kiss. Or how much he'd like to do it again. Or how he should go and apologize for his behavior. He had nothing to apologize for. He was under no obligation to go to her meeting just because she'd invited him. So why did he regret refusing?

He ate the pizza without tasting it while working up an invoice for Brody. Laughter drifted to him from the apartment next door. What were they laughing at? He shook his head. None of his business. And he wasn't feeling left out. Nope. Not at all.

His phone dinged with an incoming text and he jumped on it.

The text was from an old school friend he'd bumped into when he'd picked up his pizza yesterday. He was at the courts and asking if he'd like to play some basketball. Normally, he'd say no, but maybe this was just what he needed to get out of his own head.

Radar wasn't too happy that Gabe was leaving without him, but his owner didn't want to have to worry about his dog while playing hoops.

He'd jumped on the distraction and initially it had felt good to connect with old friends. But he'd been gone too long, seen too much to pick up where they'd left off. He realized he had more in common with new acquaintances like Brody Wilson and Des Gallagher than the guys he'd hung out with in school. The fact Brody and Des had both seen action was responsible for their instant brotherhood.

But he'd joked around and shot some hoops. He

might even have gone with them for beers after the game if he hadn't twisted his knee.

He'd laughed off falling on his butt when the knee gave out but still used it as an excuse to skip extending the evening. He pulled his Jeep back into his driveway, cut the engine and grimaced. Opening the driver's door, he inhaled and swung his legs out of the vehicle. He tested his left knee by putting weight on it and swore when pain shot through the entire leg. His knee felt similar to the time he'd sprained his ACL. He didn't think— No, make that he *hoped* that wasn't the problem. Although it hurt like hell, it wasn't quite that bad.

He slowly made his way into the house, hoping the old lady across the street wasn't watching. He didn't need the whole town knowing how stupid he was for playing in a pickup game and getting injured at his age. Huh, maybe that had put up the weird invisible barrier between him and his old friends. Was it his experiences that made him feel so much older than those guys?

Radar greeted him at the door and whined when he shut it. Great. The dog probably needed to go out and relieve himself.

"My stupidity isn't your fault. I'll let you into the backyard, but don't go far."

He laboriously limped through the house and into the kitchen. If he hadn't been rude to Addie, maybe he would have spent the evening with her and Teddy.

"Make it quick," Gabe told the dog as he opened the back door and switched on the spotlight that was supposed to illuminate the area. Nothing happened. He groaned and said a few words that would have had him filling Teddy's swear jar.

Fixing that light was one of the things on his list of repairs. Unfortunately, it involved climbing the ladder to reach the bulb attached to the highest peak on the corner of the building. About all he was able to do at the moment was shuffle around. He was hardly the role model that someone like Addie and Teddy deserved in their lives.

Radar bounded out the door, his nose to the ground. Then he raced to the edge of the yard near the trees that backed up to the property line.

"Great." Gabe leaned against the doorjamb, trying to keep his weight off his now-throbbing leg. Story of his life. He had no one to blame but himself. It was his responsibility to change the light. He'd been responsible for Tracy's pregnancy. Same with Tom. He'd been the senior officer and could have ordered Tom to stay with the vehicle. He'd been blaming the flip of a coin, but it was ultimately his fault.

Sighing, he called for the dog and received an answering bark. He whistled a few moments later with no response. What was causing Radar to ignore his commands? He couldn't handle a misbehaving dog. What made him think he would be a good influence on an impressionable boy like Teddy?

* * *

"Addie, did you hear that?" Teddy asked, getting up and going to the back door to look out.

"What, sweetie?" She finished loading the dishwasher, added detergent and latched it shut.

"I think I heard Radar barking. Out in the backyard."

She went to stand next to him and put her arms on his shoulders. "It's possible. He lives here. Gabe might have let him out to relieve himself."

"You mean, to take a whiz?" he asked, giving her a mischievous look.

"Where in the world did you hear that?" She pushed his shoulder.

He grinned and ducked his head. "At school. A lot of the kids say it."

"Well, it's not very nice."

"What do you want me to say? Take a—"

"Don't you dare." She shook her head. Was this what she had to look forward to, raising a boy? Would Gabe have known how to handle this? And why was she thinking in terms of his help? He might enjoy kissing her—and she believed he did—but that was a far cry from wanting to step up and take responsibility for a seven-year-old boy. "Let's not talk about going to the toilet at all right now."

"But you said I could ask you anything."

"And you can. And you did, and I answered." She sighed and pushed him toward the table. "Finish your homework if you want to watch TV before bed."

"But you didn't say what I could say."

"You can say he's using the bathroom."

"But Radar is outside, not—"

A knock at the back door interrupted him. "Maybe it's Mr. Gabe and Radar."

Teddy had the door open before she could react.

It was indeed Gabe and he looked a little worse for wear. His pallor was a bit gray and he had deep grooves around his mouth. She started to reach out but pulled back. If he was in pain, and she believed he was or had been, she wanted to comfort him, but would he accept it or push her away? He'd pushed her away once tonight; she wasn't sure if she had the strength to put herself out there again.

"Come in. Is Radar with you?" Teddy stuck his head out the door.

Gabe nodded and limped in holding on to the doorjamb.

Unable to help it, she rushed to his side. "What happened? Are you okay?"

He nodded. "A reminder that I'm getting too old to play pickup basketball."

"Do you need anything? What can I do?" She realized she'd been trying to herd him inside and he was resisting, albeit shakily. She had to remind herself she was not responsible for taking care of Gabe, no matter how much she felt the urge to do so.

He sucked in a breath. "I'm not here about me. It's Radar. I don't suppose there's any twenty-four-hour emergency vets in town."

"Why? What happened to him?"

Teddy pulled his head back in. "Is Radar okay?"

Gabe massaged the back of his neck. "He got into something he should've left alone."

Her mind filled with all sorts of horrors, just like it had the time Teddy said he'd almost run into the street. She hated the thought of anything happening to the dog. Being afraid was not the same as not liking the animals, though. She didn't want to see Radar *or* Gabe come to harm.

Gabe put his palm against the wall, obviously needing the support. "Come."

Radar came to the open doorway. For a moment, she didn't register what she was seeing. The dog's snout was full of porcupine quills. He slowly swung his head back and forth trying to dislodge them.

"The poor thing," she said, her stomach tightening in sympathy for the poor creature.

"Do they hurt?" Teddy asked.

Gabe nodded. "I'm sure they do. Don't touch him. I don't want those quills getting worked in any farther."

"Are you gonna pull them out?" Teddy asked, and Radar whined.

Gabe shook his head. "I think that's a job best left

to a professional. I understand it's not as straightforward as it seems."

"Oh my God, he looks so pitiful." Addie cupped her palm over her mouth and shivered. "I think he's going to need sedation."

"Why?" Teddy asked.

"Because if he jerks while they're trying to remove them, he might break the quills. The quills are actually designed to work their way in deeper, so they need to be taken out in one smooth pull with pliers. They can migrate to other parts of the body." Sometimes she hated her encyclopedic brain.

"Who designed them?" Teddy scrunched up his face.

"Mother Nature, I guess," she said.

"What happens if they do break?"

"The vet will need to switch to sanitized tweezers to..." Her voice trailed off and she glanced up.

Gabe shifted his stance. "This is all my fault. I trusted Radar to come straight back, but he's still a dog and dogs chase porcupines. Damn. I spent so much time concentrating on keeping him safe from snipers and IEDs that I forgot to take into consideration the more mundane dangers lurking here at home."

"To what?" Teddy demanded.

She frowned at her brother. "To *what* what?"

Gabe cleared his throat and winced as he looked at a pathetic Radar, his snout full of quills. "I think your sister was talking about using tweezers to dig the pieces out."

"Ew," Teddy said, and he made a face. "That sounds—"

"I don't think we need to discuss this right now, Teddy." She glanced at Gabe. The poor guy looked positively queasy. Her earlier annoyance at his dismissive behavior after their kiss evaporated.

"But it's happening now," Teddy whined.

Despite the circumstances, Gabe laughed at his comment. Her gaze met Gabe's in a common understanding that they were protecting Teddy from the gory details. This silent communication passed between them as they stared at one another over his head. Was this what it was like to be intimately close to someone? Sharing moments without the need for words?

"I think your sister is getting grossed out, so maybe we can talk about it later."

"Hey, I…" Addie started to object, but Gabe winked at her and she understood what he was doing. She smirked at him and said, "I guess we'll both have something to discuss later."

"Agreed, but first I need to find emergency veterinary care."

"We don't have a twenty-four-hour— Wait. I do have Dr. Greer's personal cell number. We were on a committee together last year for the annual Independence Day celebration. I'm sure she'd be happy to help an animal in distress." She grabbed her phone off the counter and scrolled through her contacts.

"I hate to put you on the spot, but do you think you could call her?" He gave her a pleading look. "Radar didn't get into this mess by himself. I should have gone outside with him, called him back immediately when he darted off."

Radar sat, watching patiently while Addie tried to reach the vet. Her heart went out to both man and animal.

Teddy hunkered down in front of Radar, his hands between his knees, avoiding touching the dog. "Learning lessons is no fun, huh?"

Addie drew in a sharp breath. Was that what Michelle had told that little boy, a sweet child in pain, when he'd gotten burned? Oh, she had no doubt that was where that sentiment had come from. Their mother had been quick to tell her that she hoped she'd learned her lesson after she'd gotten bitten by the neighbor's dog. It was her responsibility now to undo the damage Michelle had done to Teddy—*and* to her.

Chapter Ten

Gabe shifted his weight, easing off the sore knee as much as possible to relieve the pain. Whatever his discomfort, he was pretty sure Radar was in a heck of a lot more, and that was on him for getting them into this mess. But none of that mattered now because Addie was there and willing to help, despite his earlier treatment of her.

Evidently the call had gone through, because she was speaking with someone, explaining the situation. The tension he'd been carrying in his shoulders drained away. He hoped to have the chance to make this up to her.

"Uh-huh," she said and gave him a thumbs-up.

His heart did that stumble thing he associated with Addie and he sagged against the wall. He might not be seeing his bed or even his couch as he'd planned, but at least Radar would receive the necessary treatment. He'd been fooling himself when he'd said he was honoring a promise when he brought the dog home. Truth was, Radar had burrowed deep into his heart and he'd walk to the ends of the earth to see that he was taken care of. How many times had Radar brought him out of his dark thoughts? Retrieved him from the nightmare of war and brought him back to reality without any formal training?

Addie set her phone on the counter. "She says she'll meet us at her office. She's going to try to contact her vet tech too. She mentioned he might need anesthesia when they go to get all of the quills out."

He straightened up and away from the wall, pulling out his own phone to call up the GPS. "Where is her office?"

"I know exactly where it is. Teddy, go get our jackets from the closet by the front door."

The boy sprang up, his expression hopeful. "We're going with Mr. Gabe and Radar?"

She glanced over at Gabe, her chin at a determined angle. "You don't look like you're in any state to drive yourself."

He opened his mouth to argue but closed it again.

As much as he wanted to protest, she was absolutely right, so he nodded. "Okay, but we should take my Jeep. I have a crate for Radar in the rear."

She bit her lip. "Is it a stick?"

"The car?" He shook his head. "No."

"So, I get to ride in Mr. Gabe's Jeep?" Teddy asked, as if it were some sort of treat.

"I thought I told you to go get the jackets," she said and picked up her purse from the kitchen table. "Unless you prefer I call Mrs. O to see if…"

"I figured that would get him moving," she said as Teddy ran from the room.

He marveled at how she'd kept a cool head and did what was necessary. Sure, he'd helped her with her phobia, but she wasn't miraculously cured, and yet she wasn't letting it prevent her from helping them.

"I can't thank you enough," he said, and Radar whined. Even the dog recognized how special this woman was. "Make that *we* can't thank you enough."

She waved her hand. "It's what neighbors do."

"I also owe you an apology."

"For what?"

"For earlier. I was rude when you invited me to your meeting."

"It's not *my* meeting. It happens to be held at the library and—"

"Here, Addie." Teddy came back with two jackets

and handed her one. "Mr. Gabe? Will it cost a lot of money to get Radar fixed?"

Radar whined as if the question had been weighing on him too.

"Teddy." Addie's tone held a note of warning.

"I was gonna say that maybe we should take the swear jar with us, just in case. You know, if Mr. Gabe needs extra money to help pay. If that's okay with you, Addie. You're always saying how much money it costs when you take a dog to the doctor."

Addie gave Gabe an apologetic look and opened her mouth, but before she spoke, he said, "I don't think that will be necessary, but I appreciate your generous offer." He glanced at the dog. "And I'm sure Radar appreciates it too."

"Well, we'd better go. We don't want to keep Emily waiting," Addie said and handed her car keys to Teddy. "Get your booster seat from our car so we can put it in Gabe's."

He felt a bit disoriented sitting in the passenger seat of his own vehicle, but it did feel good, being off his knee.

"Is everyone buckled in?" Addie asked before starting the Jeep.

"Yes, ma'am," Gabe said.

"Yup," came Teddy's response.

A whine from the crate in the back was Radar's reply.

Teddy giggled. "Radar answered too. Did you hear that, Mr. Gabe?"

"I certainly did." Gabe chuckled and glanced at Addie, who met his gaze before she backed out of the driveway. The gloom and doom he'd been feeling earlier had lifted; it had eased the moment Addie had asked what she could do to help.

All rational thought fled when he got lost in her sparkling eyes, which looked as if the sun were shining through them. He felt warmth flood his face. Where the heck had that corny thought come from? And at a time like this, no less?

"Mr. Gabe?"

"Yes?"

"Do you like Addie?"

"Teddy," she groaned.

"What? Last year, when I tol' you I liked Ashley Cook from my school, you said I should tell her."

"Yes, but…" She stopped at the end of their street and waited for traffic before pulling out.

What was he supposed to say to a seven-year-old? "Yes, I have feelings for your sister, but they're not exactly appropriate, at least not enough to admit to a young boy about his sister"?

"Well, to answer your question. Yes, Teddy, I like your sister," he said and paused before adding, "Very much, in fact."

Now he'd gone and done it. Home less than a

month and admitting to having feelings for a woman. And not just any woman, but one who was responsible for an impressionable boy. Returning to Loon Lake, he hadn't intended to live a celibate life, but this was definitely not what he'd planned either.

"That's good 'cause Addie likes you."

"Teddy," she said in a pained tone.

Gabe arched an eyebrow and looked over at her. "Is that true?"

She briefly took her eyes from the road to look at him. "Yes," she said shortly and shifted her concentration back to her driving.

"See?" Teddy leaned back in his seat. "It worked. Just like with Ashley Cook."

"Yes, it, uh, did," Gabe said and bit the inside of his cheek to keep from laughing. When he could talk without chuckling, he said, *"And a little child shall lead them."*

"Huh?" came from the back seat.

"Nothing," they both responded at the same time.

He had a feeling Teddy's definition of liking was a bit different from his. His encompassed a whole range, from lustful thoughts to enjoying sitting on the front stoop with her and talking about everything and nothing.

Addie switched on the blinker and pulled into the turn lane.

"We're here," she said, sounding relieved as she drove into the parking lot.

The veterinarian's office was located in a newer one-story, detached building with a brick facade and white-painted trim. Addie parked the car next to the door.

A petite woman wearing a white lab coat over light green scrubs met them at the entrance. Her long blond hair was pulled back into a ponytail. The pin under the front pocket said Dr. Emily Greer, DVM.

"Thank you so much for meeting us," Addie said as they embraced.

"I'm glad I was able to come," the vet replied.

Teddy ran up to her. "Hi! Remember me?"

Dr. Greer gave him a hug too. "Of course I remember you, Teddy. You came last year with your sister to the July Fourth celebration and helped me set up my booth."

"Radar came all the way from Afghanistan," Teddy told her.

The vet grinned. "My, my, he came a long way."

"Oh, he didn't come today." He shook his head. "He came a long time ago. At least two weeks, huh, Mr. Gabe?"

"At least two weeks," Gabe said, grateful Teddy had distracted them while he practically crawled out of the car. Not good for his manly image.

Addie introduced Gabe to the vet, and they exchanged pleasantries.

"I guess I'd better meet the patient."

* * *

Gabe switched off the ball game on TV when Radar abandoned his post on the couch to run to the front door. It had been three days since their injuries, and both were healing nicely. Radar more so than him, since Gabe was still limping a bit—like now as he followed the dog to the door.

Dr. Greer had removed all the quills without any breaking, so she hadn't had to resort to digging any out with tweezers.

Gabe was using the RICE method of rest, ice, compression and elevation to take care of his knee, and it was responding.

"You'd tell me if it was someone other than Teddy, wouldn't you, boy?" he said to the dog as he reached for the knob.

Gabe laughed when Radar gave him a look that said he knew his job. Sure enough, Teddy was on the other side, his hand poised to knock. Gabe's chest swelled at the sight. He looked forward to the boy's company as much as he enjoyed Addie's.

So why had he done little to encourage seeing her except in passing in the days following their emergency trip to the vet? Sure, he'd been staying off his feet to heal his knee, but that was only part of it. Had it been because he'd admitted liking her? Or worse yet, her admitting she liked him? Which was scarier?

Oh man, thoughts like that just illustrated how deep his feelings went.

"How did you know I was here?" the boy asked as Gabe opened up.

"Radar told me."

"He did?" The boy giggled and hugged Radar. "How'd he do that? He can't talk."

Wanna bet? Gabe grinned and replied, "He came to the door to let me know you were here."

Teddy scrunched up his face. "But I didn't even get to knock before you opened it."

"True, but dogs hear better than we do," he told Teddy. "They hear sounds four times farther away than we do, so he must've heard you coming."

Teddy slowly shook his head. "Now you sound like Addie."

Gabe laughed. "I'll take that as a compliment."

"Huh?"

"Nothing. I— What have you got in your pocket? Radar keeps trying to stick his nose in it."

The boy put his hand in his hoodie and held up a clear sandwich bag with cookies shaped like bones. "Look what I made."

"You baked those?" Gabe smiled but wasn't sure where this was heading.

"Yup. Well, Addie helped. Can I give one to Radar?"

Radar threw Gabe a hopeful look and whined.

"I don't normally let him have human food, but I guess one won't hurt. They don't have chocolate or raisins, do they?" Did Addie even know Teddy had brought the cookies over? She knew chocolate was toxic for dogs and would never willingly feed it to Radar. She might be afraid of dogs, but she would never harm one.

"No. Addie looked up a bunch of dog recipes and used the best one."

"Dog recipes? You mean those are dog cookies?"

"Yeah, but Addie says it's okay for people to eat them too. I tried one and it was kinda yucky." He made a face. "I told her they were pretty bad, but she said it won't kill me. And she said dogs' taste buds are different than ours."

"These aren't really cookies but dog biscuits?"

The boy held the bag up. Radar sat at Teddy's feet, his eyes on the bag. "You can try one if you want. I did."

"So you say, but I think I'll pass." Gabe chuckled, but Addie's gesture made all sorts of mushy stuff happen in his chest. Truth was, he'd missed their company and was through avoiding spending quality time with them. "Why did you and your sister make these?"

"I asked if we could buy some for Radar, and she said making them would be more special. She said it's like when I make stuff during art at school or when the library has arts and crafts. She says she likes those cards better than store-bought." Teddy paused for breath and opened the bag. "Do you think that means they're more special? Do you think Radar will think they're more special?"

"I'm sure Radar will enjoy the ones you baked for him." And Gabe wouldn't be rude enough to refuse them as he had with the cupcakes. He'd sooner eat a dog biscuit than hurt the kid's feelings. And he'd do anything to protect the boy. It didn't matter that he wasn't his own flesh and blood. This bond went deeper than duty.

"Addie says if Radar likes them, we'll fix more for her library thing."

"She's going to feed dog biscuits to the library patrons?"

"Well…they are homemade."

"But—"

Teddy burst out laughing. "Gotcha!"

It seemed the kid had a sense of humor. "Very clever."

"Not really. I said the same thing you did to Addie, and that's what she said. I didn't make it up myself. Can I give one to Radar?"

"Sure. Hold it on your open palm and let him take it."

Teddy did as he was told, and Radar looked to Gabe, his tongue hanging out of the side of his mouth. He put the dog out of his misery and nodded. Radar gently removed the treat from Teddy's hand and wolfed it down in two bites.

"He liked it." Teddy held up the bag. "Addie said

not to give him too many. She said that was for you to decide. You will let him have more, won't you, Mr. Gabe?"

"I will." He nodded solemnly and accepted the bag. "What is your sister doing today?"

"She's cleaning up the mess we made in the kitchen baking the dog biscuits." Teddy hunkered down to pet Radar. "Did you watch any videos about making a race car for Cub Scouts?"

Teddy was looking at him as expectantly as Radar had the bag of homemade dog treats. Although he'd never been a Scout himself, he now knew about all there was to know about the Pinewood Derby. It was a toss-up who was more excited, him or Teddy.

"I did. And I need to be sure I have all the things we'll need before we start building it."

"You mean it? You'll really help me?" Teddy asked, and Gabe nodded. "It's spring break, so I don't have school next week. Do you think we could do it then?"

"I think that can be arranged. Will you be home every day?"

He nodded enthusiastically. "Addie says she's taking vacation days so I don't have to go to the library with her or stay with that Mrs. O'Malley. I told Addie I was old enough to stay by myself, but she says no. What do you think, Mr. Gabe?"

Knowing better than to get in the middle of that,

he held up his hands. "I think your sister knows best."

"My mom used to leave me alone, and I was just a little kid then."

Gabe was at a loss for words. What could he say to the boy? That his mother had been irresponsible and Addie was anything but?

"My mom says if I go back to live with her, she promises not to do that again, but she breaks her promises. You won't tell Addie I said that, will you?"

"Well, I—"

"I think our mom likes to break her promises, 'cause she does it all the time."

Gabe shifted in discomfort. "Have you talked to your sister about that?"

He shook his head. "I think Addie believes her because she says Mom can't help it because she's sick. But I'm not a baby. I know she does bad things."

"I think you need to talk to your sister about this."

"I can't."

"Why not?" Gabe asked.

"'Cause it's like when a little kid believes in the Easter Bunny or the tooth fairy. I'm not supposed to tell the adults I know something's a lie."

"Well, I'm not sure it's exactly the same thing. Your sister is an adult," he reminded Teddy.

"I'll think about it, but I don't want to ruin anything for her. Can Radar and I play ball now? Addie says if I do, she'll come and sit on the steps to watch us."

"Sure." And he could sit on the steps with Addie. God, he must have it bad, when lounging on the front stoop with a woman sounded like fun. Huh, it must've been longer than he'd realized since he'd been with someone.

In between deployments, after his pa had died, he'd stayed on base, hung out with other marines. He'd gone out with women, but those few times could be best described as hookups, nothing resembling a proper relationship.

"Mr. Gabe?"

"I'll put the biscuits away for now. I bought Radar a Frisbee. Would you like to play with that instead of the ball?"

"Okay. Can you show me how to throw it?"

"Sure thing, bud." If someone had told him that he would enjoy showing a seven-year-old how best to throw a Frisbee, he would have thought they were nuts. But being able to share things with Teddy gave him a good feeling. It was not the same as serving his country but important nonetheless.

He may not have appreciated it enough, but his pa had always been there for him, even when he'd messed up and gotten into trouble as a teen. Sure, the old man hadn't lectured, but he'd taken the time to set him straight. He might not have had all the newest gadgets or expensive clothes like the other boys, but his pa had given him what mattered. And now he found he wanted to do that for Teddy. Give him the gift of time, listen to him and let the boy know he was important.

He'd just finished giving Frisbee-throwing pointers when Addie came onto the front stoop. He limped over to the chairs she'd already set up. Radar and Teddy both paused in their game of fetch. Radar's tongue lolled out of the side of his mouth, and Gabe swore the dog wore a smug expression. *Oh man, Bishop, you are losing it.*

"Addie, look. We're playing Frisbee. Mr. Gabe taught us."

"I see that, sweetie."

Addie looked at Gabe and her heart melted. He'd been so patient with Teddy. She needed to be careful or she'd be falling for her neighbor. If it wasn't already too late. Which did not make sense, because she barely knew him.

She noticed he made a face as he lowered himself into the chair.

"How's the knee?"

"Getting better," Gabe replied, adding, "I made a pact with Radar. He's to stay away from porcupines, and I'll refrain from playing basketball."

She loved his sense of humor. "How about a game of trivia instead?"

He raised an eyebrow. "Right now?"

"Unless you can't handle it."

"Bring it."

"You ready?" She rubbed her fingers on her chest and blew on them.

"What two countries share the longest international border?"

"The US and Canada. *Pfft*. You can do better than that." He puffed up his chest and motioned toward his pecs with his open hands. "Get rough. I can take it."

But could she? She remembered those calluses on his hands and wondered what they would feel like in certain other places on her body. *Get back into the game*, she ordered herself. "Who wrote *The Silence of the Lambs*?"

"Look at you. Going all librarian on me." He narrowed his eyes and studied her. "Thomas Harris. Now, how about I quiz you? I like to know exactly what *I'm* getting into."

"Bring it, Marine." She lifted her chin.

"When does the Marine Corps celebrate its birthday?"

"November tenth." She blew on her fingertips.

After playing several more rounds and calling it a draw, Gabe said, "Teddy tells me he's off school next week."

"He is."

"Maybe the three of us could do something. Go

for pizza, maybe take Teddy to indoor miniature golf. I think he'd like that."

And so would I. That sounded just fine to her—in fact, more than fine. It sounded like a plan.

The next day was unseasonably warm, so when Teddy dropped by to see if he could help with anything, Gabe suggested they wash the Jeep together. He sensed that Teddy wanted to talk about something.

Although he hadn't thought about it at the time, washing his pa's old heap with him hadn't done a thing to improve its appearance. Washing it had been an excuse to spend time together and for Pa to impart wisdom without appearing to lecture.

"Everyone says you got medals and stuff for bravery in Afghanistan," the boy muttered.

"It's true I was awarded a distinguished service medal, but I was just doing what the marines taught me." Gabe increased pressure as he rubbed the soapy sponge over the hood and side panels. What was he supposed to say to the kid? The last thing he wanted was to glorify war, but neither did he want to lie. "I'm not sure I'd call doing my job being brave, though."

"Oh." Teddy's shoulders slumped, and he scuffed the ground with the toe of his sneaker.

"Why did you ask, bud?"

Teddy lifted his bony shoulders and let them drop. "I thought maybe you could teach me."

"To be brave?"

The kid nodded.

"What makes you think you're not already?"

Gabe thought about the burn scars on the boy's hands and arms but didn't want to call attention to them. Did the other kids pick on him for that? Gabe knew firsthand how cruel other children could be. He recalled the first time someone teased him because he didn't have a mother. As if he were to blame for her death when he was six. Teddy was staring at his feet. Did he get teased for living with his sister? "Have kids been bullying you for something?"

"Not me but my friend Sam. Some bigger kids called him 'dummy' because he can't talk." Teddy shrugged again. "It's not his fault. He got hit by a car when he was really little, and that's how come he can't talk. But he's a real good LEGO builder."

Gabe nodded, proud of Teddy for befriending Des and Natalie's son, Sam. Before spending time with Teddy, he wouldn't have thought it possible to feel like this about a boy who wasn't his biological son. He had to swallow to dislodge the lump in his throat before he could speak. "You don't need to talk to assemble LEGO bricks, huh?"

Teddy's face brightened. "Yeah. He put together an airport set all by hisself, and he's real good at finding the pieces we need in the big bucket."

"Did you tell your teacher about the other boys?"

He shook his head vigorously. "They said if I snitched, they'd know it. Addie says that if you stand up to bullies, they will back down. But girls sure are different, ya know what I mean?"

Gabe cleared his throat to stop the laugh that threatened to emerge. "I think I do, bud. Can you get the hose and hand it to me?" Gabe pointed to where he'd left the implement. He felt as though he were tiptoeing his way through a minefield. He was honored Teddy had come to him, but he worried about saying the wrong thing. What did he know about giving advice to a kid, really? Would he have automatically known what to say if his own son had lived? Would having raised him from infancy given him special insight, or would he have the same fear of messing up, saying the wrong thing?

Teddy ran over to the hose and picked it up by the nozzle and handed it over. "Girls say mean things and pull each other's hair and stuff, but us guys don't do that, do we?"

"Sometimes, bud. But I don't think your sister wants you to get in trouble for fighting either. I could give you tips on how to defend yourself if someone tries to start a fight with you."

Teddy shrugged. "I learned to do that pretty good in one of the places I went to before I came to live with Addie."

Gabe winced at Teddy's matter-of-fact tone. They

had a lot in common, because circumstances had made both of them vulnerable as children. In very different ways, of course. He had never been in any physical danger, just suffering dented pride at having to accept charity. Teddy, however, had suffered much worse and had the scars to prove it. What else had the boy been through in his relatively short life? No wonder Addie was so protective. "Okay. Then what are you asking me?"

"Teach me how to be brave. Whenever I stand up to those bigger kids, I feel… I feel…" He glanced around as if afraid someone would hear him. "I'm scared."

"Being brave doesn't mean you're not scared. Hel—" He cut himself off before he swore, adding, "*Heck*, I was scared most of the time in Afghanistan."

The boy's eyes grew larger behind the lenses of his glasses. "You were?"

Gabe nodded and adjusted the nozzle. "Being scared has nothing to do with bravery, Teddy. Sounds like you were being courageous when you stood up for your friend Sam."

"How was I brave if I was scared the whole time?" Teddy shook his head and hunched his shoulders forward.

"Facing your fears and not giving in to them is what being brave is about."

Teddy scowled. "How can that be true, if you're afraid at all?"

Gabe waved the hose back and forth to rinse the soapsuds off the side of the Jeep. "You said you were afraid, but you still stood up to the boys picking on your friend. I tell you, Teddy, that's the definition of bravery."

Teddy thought for a moment, then smiled. "For real?"

"For real."

Gabe was glad he could help the kid. It gave him a good feeling.

Except what he felt was a heck of a lot more complicated. *Good* didn't even begin to describe his feelings for Teddy and his sister. *Complicated* with a big *C* was more like it.

He was wading into deep water and couldn't be sure of keeping his head above it. If he drowned, he could take Addie and Teddy with him.

Hurting either of them was the last thing he wanted.

Chapter Eleven

Addie put up the Tea & Talk sign she'd laminated on the door of the community room. The meeting was held at the library on a monthly basis, although the name alternated. The vote to name the group had been deadlocked, with no one wanting to give an inch. She laughed. It was nice to think that was one of the most controversial things in her life. She'd been the one who'd come up with the compromise. Every once in a while, she'd put up the wrong sign to see if anyone noticed. Someone always did and called her out on it. She'd act like it had been an honest mistake and correct her error, secretly chuckling to herself.

Despite the hot tempers over the name, good things were accomplished by the group. They discussed projects that benefited the residents of the town. At Christmas, they decorated an "angel tree" at the library, where children were allowed to hang holiday wishes. Then benefactors would select a paper angel and fulfill what was written on it. The majority of the messages were from underprivileged children or from parents who couldn't afford to give presents that year to their youngsters. But the library also partnered with adult social services to grant the wishes of elderly people with limited means or no close relatives.

With the porcupine incident and school break behind her, she'd given up trying to interest Gabe in today's meeting. They'd been getting along so well she didn't want any controversies to threaten their budding friendship. She had to admit, at least to herself in the dead of the night when she couldn't sleep, how much she'd grown to care about Gabe in such a short time.

What if he didn't share her growing feelings? Or panicked and pushed her away? She needed to protect Teddy from getting hurt if he grew too attached to Gabe. The children always suffered when the adults mismanaged their relationships. She didn't want her brother to become collateral damage.

She'd just set a stack of the minutes she'd printed out from last month's gathering on a small table by the door when someone bumped into her. It was her friend Natalie.

"You were deep in thought." Natalie grinned. "Does it have anything to do with what's been happening with you and our war hero?"

Addie tried to act innocent. "What do you mean?"

"I heard you and Teddy were seen with Gabe at the pizza parlor. And that he and Teddy were playing video games."

Addie cursed her light complexion. She didn't need to see a mirror to know she was blushing like some schoolgirl. "Well, he does live next door to me, so our being seen together isn't exactly notable."

Except it was more than that and she was worried. What if Gabe didn't share her growing feelings? Was she strong enough to protect her and Teddy from heartbreak? Teddy wasn't the only one who'd fallen in love. She drew in a sharp breath. Oh my God, she'd fallen in love with Gabe. It was too late for both of them and she—

"Earth to Addie. Are you even listening to me?" Natalie bumped her again. "I said that's not what I heard."

"What? What have you heard?"

"You were seen playing mini golf, and I also heard something about you and him at the vet. For someone who doesn't like dogs, you going with him to Dr. Greer seems like something."

"I told you I don't dislike dogs… I just exercise a

healthy dose of caution around them." But not even she believed that statement at this point.

"Uh-huh," Natalie said and made a noise in her throat.

Addie sighed. "Gabe's dog and Teddy have bonded." And she and Gabe had bonded, too...like she never had with a man before.

"Considering how hot Gabe is, I'd say that's fantastic. Gives you an excuse to hang out. Or am I missing something?"

"You're not missing anything. It's a good thing, Teddy spending time with a guy like Gabe and a dog like Radar."

"So?"

"I'm not sure getting involved with someone right now is in our best interest." That was her go-to excuse. Like telling Teddy they couldn't afford a dog. She could count the number of dates, let alone actual relationships, she'd had on one hand.

Probably accounts for the reason you're still a virgin.

"Because of the upcoming custody hearing?"

"Yeah." Not to mention the whole I'm-still-a-virgin thing. Admitting her fear of dogs was one thing. Admitting she was like some old maid from one of those historical romances her Harlequin ladies were always checking out was another matter. She wasn't even quite sure how she'd gotten to be twenty-three and not done it. Maybe thinking in euphemistic terms like *done it* would explain it. She felt like some sort of throwback, and she didn't even have the threat of being labeled with a scarlet letter as an excuse.

Admitting her cynophobia to Gabe was hard enough… Imagine admitting this! What would he think of her? Would he finally see her as too young and put an end to their growing friendship? How would that affect Teddy? Her little brother would hate to be cut off from Radar and Gabe.

"Maybe you being in a relationship would help you relax and open up a bit," Natalie suggested.

"Being married or engaged might, but shacking up with my neighbor, not so much."

Natalie clucked her tongue. "Well, sure, when you put it like that…"

"How else would I put it? Besides, my first responsibility is to Teddy." She refused to have boyfriends or even father figures coming in and out of his life. She didn't want him growing up thinking that was how men behaved around women. Sure, not all relationships succeeded, but having revolving-door ones wasn't what she wanted to teach him either.

"Not to the extent that you should forgo having a life for yourself. We all make sacrifices for our children, but self-martyrdom isn't going to help anyone."

"I know, but not all of us can easily find a great guy like Des." How hard had she actually looked? Even when their mom wasn't using, a lot of the care for Teddy had fallen on her. Or had Addie simply used their mother's addiction as an excuse after seeing so many unhealthy attachments? She had to admit that going on a few casual dates would hardly harm Teddy or give him the wrong idea.

Natalie hooked her arm through Addie's and sighed. "He is pretty wonderful."

Addie laughed and nodded. Her friend was definitely smitten with the former naval lieutenant. Somehow Natalie and Sam had managed to turn the town scrooge into a family man. They even ran a successful hippotherapy business on their farm on the edge of town.

Natalie pulled out a covered container from the tote bag she had and opened the cover.

Addie looked up from measuring grounds into the coffeepot, her mouth already watering. "Ooh, what did you bring this month?"

"I baked some cranberry bars."

"And Des didn't eat them all?" Addie knew Natalie's husband had a sweet tooth.

"Ha! I had to make a double batch or he wouldn't have let me out of the house."

"He isn't coming?" She set the coffee to brew.

"No. He's still swamped with orders for his crushed glass ornaments." Natalie pulled out a seat. "What's on the agenda for today?"

"Expansion of our shut-in meals program." Addie sat next to her friend.

"Are there people we've missed?"

"Not people but pets. What if we expanded it to include their animals too?"

People started filing into the meeting. After greetings were exchanged and everyone sat, Addie began explaining the suggested program revisions.

"You want to bring meals for dogs?" someone asked.

Addie grinned. "Not meals. Dog and cat food. We could bring dry and canned."

"What made you think of this?"

Addie shook her head. "I didn't really think of it myself... I read an article about it and thought it was a good idea. The piece I saw was about dogs, but I think we should include cats. I know some of our seniors have both." In reality, though, she knew what had sparked the idea. *Gabe and Radar.*

Marian Benedetti, an avid cozy-mystery reader, with a preference for the ones having covers featuring cats, lifted her eyebrows at Addie, a smile playing about her mouth. "So, this has nothing to do with a certain hunky hero being seen around town with a dog?"

"Absolutely not." Uh-oh. She may as well have announced to these meddling ladies that she had the hots for Gabe. Yeah, the skepticism around the table was palpable now. "Gabe isn't a senior citizen, nor does he need anyone's help to feed his dog."

"Oh, on a first-name basis, are we?"

Of course we are. We're both adults and this isn't

a Jane Austen novel. The sarcastic reply came bubbling up, but she clamped her lips around it. She didn't want to alienate any of these people, even though she did wish they'd mind their own business.

She drew in a calming breath. "As I was saying, I know Ogle helps deliver meals to people who can't make it to the weekly luncheons at the church. I'm sure he wouldn't mind taking dog or cat food too."

A few people asked questions and Addie made some notes. "We'll talk to him. We should check with Pastor Cook. We might be missing some seniors, or there may be some who feed themselves but could benefit from the extra help with pet food. I've noticed some people boxing up some of their meal at the weekly luncheons at the church. I always thought it was so they could have the leftovers for supper or the next day, but I sometimes wonder how many save some of it for their pets."

"See what you started? And I thought you didn't like dogs." Natalie playfully bumped shoulders with Addie.

Addie felt heat rise in her face. "It's not that."

Since confessing to Gabe about her fear of dogs, she didn't feel as embarrassed to admit it aloud. Gabe didn't laugh or pity her. Instead, he helped her. Like they were comrades in arms—or partners in life. When Natalie gave her a questioning look, Addie shrugged. "I was bitten as a kid and have carried a fear of dogs ever since."

Natalie nodded, her expression understanding. "That's understandable."

It was, wasn't it? Why had she always tried to keep her phobia a secret? Maybe it had more to do with what had happened *after*—her mother's response to her injury—than the actual dog bite. The attack had made her afraid of canines, but what had happened as a result had made her afraid to admit the weakness. Because of her injuries, social services had been called. Addie had felt the need to take on the burden of responsibility for having her and her mom come under such scrutiny. As if admitting things or asking for help was wrong. Maybe it was time to place the guilt where it belonged. With Michelle, who was the parent.

Addie shook her head to clear her thoughts and listened as Ellie McBride talked about helping the seniors at the skilled nursing facility feel more involved in town activities.

"Maybe we can have a weekly activity session at the library. Addie?"

"You mean like the story hour we have for the kids?" She began making notes as Ellie explained her ideas.

A disturbance caused Addie to glance up from her note taking. Gabe hovered in the doorway, looking around hesitantly at everyone. The pencil in her hand snapped in half as their eyes met across the room. Did she possess the ability to hide her newly acknowledged feelings of love, or was it written all over her face?

Natalie leaned closer. "I thought you said he wasn't coming."

"That's what he told me," Addie whispered back.

Gabe paused before entering the room. Did he really want to join them? He was doing this because, as much as he'd hated being the object of charity as a kid, the people of Loon Lake were kind, generous people, and ignoring them now that he didn't need their help would be rude. But he'd considered staying home because he didn't want the attention or the exposure.

Yeah, okay, Addie had wanted him to get involved. Coming to the meeting had nothing to do with the disappointment that had briefly shadowed her eyes when he'd refused her invitation. He'd remembered she'd worn the same expression when he'd turned away the cupcakes.

What was it about her and her expressive blue eyes that made him want to avoid disappointing her? It wasn't as if he owed her anything. But he had to admit to himself that something about being with her and Teddy had softened his heart. He wanted to spend as much time with them as possible, even if that meant getting more involved with the town and their nosy neighbors.

Before he could retreat, Ogle Whatley had spotted him and was heading across the room toward him. Too late to turn back now. As well as owning Loon Lake General Store with his wife, Tavie, Ogle owned the local towing and repair garage.

"So good to see you back safe and sound, son." Ogle grabbed him in one of those guy hugs. Letting go and stepping back, the older man said, "Glad you could make it to the meeting. Our Addie didn't think you were going to be here. She mentioned that you've been busy with repairs and upgrades to Grace Pierce's place."

Gabe frowned, trying to place the name.

"Grace was Natalie's grandmother. She left the place to Natalie when she passed away," Addie said as she came to stand next to him, bringing her fresh scent with her. He still hadn't quite figured out how she always smelled like grapefruit. Shampoo, maybe? Whatever it was, it had him spellbound.

"Sorry I haven't gotten over to see you since you've been back," Ogle was saying.

"That's okay. I wouldn't have expected you to go out of your way."

"As much as your dad helped me, coming to see you was the least I could do. Of course, I may have ulterior motives."

"My pa helped you out?" Why didn't he know about this?

"I like to keep my eye on some of our vets and offer up what I can whenever necessary. Your dad started by repairing a snowblower for one of my Korean vets. Then when a case of gout curtailed some of my activities, he took over my route."

"Route?" He tried to recall his pa mentioning any of this and couldn't. Guilt burned in his gut that he hadn't made the effort to get home more often before his father had passed away. He owed his pa for trying his best as a single parent. It was too late to repay his father, but maybe he could pay it forward in another way.

"Not everyone can make it to the weekly luncheons for one reason or another, and I make it a point to deliver a meal. Not to mention the missions Tavie sends me on. Your dad took over those missions too."

"He did?"

Ogle nodded. "He was the first person she called to help when she needed it."

Gabe straightened his shoulders. Knowing his pa had been someone people turned to for help filled him with pride. "I didn't realize how involved he was."

"Yeah, he said how proud he was of what you were doing and wanted to help out our veterans. I sure do miss him."

"So do I."

Ogle clapped him on the shoulder. "Like I said, he preened like a peacock over your service and all that you did."

Despite the sudden thickening in his throat, the tightness in his chest eased. Maybe he hadn't disappointed his pa after all.

"Too bad your dad won't be here for the parade, but I know how proud he was of you."

Gabe swallowed. Ogle's expression was open and honest. Had his pa gotten over his initial disappointment at his son picking the military over—? Wait. "What parade?"

Ogle chuckled, his Santa Claus–like belly jiggling. "We still have a parade for Memorial Day, and of course you're going to be our grand marshal."

"I am?" He groaned.

This was exactly why he hadn't wanted to come to this meeting. Nor did he want to get involved. All this hero talk made him uncomfortable. Anything he'd done was far from heroic. He couldn't even take credit for Radar. Tom was the one who'd rescued the dog and had even devised the plan to bring him to the US. All Gabe had done was honor his friend's dying wish.

Guilt ate at him to think he was enjoying the companionship and comfort from Radar when it was Tom who should be doing it. And he'd left his wife for the military after they'd lost their child. Was that the behavior of a hero?

Addie and Teddy should watch out; he was bound

to let them down too. No matter how much he was coming to care for them both.

Gabe stayed to help Addie clean up after the meeting. She appreciated his presence and the fact he'd stuck around.

"I have to admit I was shocked when you showed up," she said as she locked the room.

He shrugged. "I gave it some thought and decided you had a point. If I'm going to be around for a while, I should try and assimilate."

"I'm glad you came."

He smiled, warmth flooding his body at her words. "I got to see your official librarian persona."

"I guess I need to confess that I'm only a library assistant, since I haven't graduated yet. I quit after my first year. But I'm taking online classes."

"What made you want to be a librarian?"

"I always considered the library to be my sanctuary when I was a kid. And I wanted to be able to give other kids, and everyone else in the community, that type of positive experience."

Gabe felt the sting of guilt at how he'd grown up, not regarding his home as a sanctuary but instead feeling ashamed of where they'd lived. That front yard full of dirt, weeds and rusting hulks. At least his home, as embarrassing as it might have been for him, had never been a place to fear or feel unsafe, like theirs was for Addie and Teddy. His pa may have struggled with low-paying jobs, but he had never raised his hand in anger at his son or abandoned him to use drugs. As a matter of fact, since his return, Gabe realized he was seeing his father in a whole new light. Instead of being an object of scorn or pity as Gabe had always feared, his dad had been genuinely liked and admired by the residents of Loon Lake. And rather than just accepting charity, his father had worked hard to give back to the community and veterans. Gabe now felt ashamed of his feelings back then. But even though he couldn't change his past, he knew he could change his future—maybe be like his pa, going from taking help in the past to giving back now.

"Were…?" He cleared his throat and started again. "Were things always so bad for you as a kid?"

"Only when she was using. There were times when she'd get clean, and things would be good for a while. But she always had trouble finding a job that paid enough, so we tended to live in sketchy areas."

"You didn't grow up in Loon Lake?"

"No. Nothing like this. I used to pass by streets like this one and wish I could live there."

Welcome to the club, he thought, but said, "You must be proud that you can bring Teddy up in a place like this."

"Yes, I was so relieved to get the job here. Everyone said I could make more money working at a bigger library, but for me, it wouldn't be worth it. Despite what I sometimes say, I consider Loon Lake a wonderful place." She glanced at him, her cheeks dusted with pink. "Although, I guess if you're looking for trouble, you can find it, even in a place like this."

"Ah, I see some of my youthful transgressions have been discussed."

"They didn't keep you out of the marines, so I have to assume they weren't that bad. Or you simply didn't get caught."

He grinned. "Maybe a little of both."

"Is that supposed to make me feel better?" she said.

"It doesn't?"

She sighed. "I know you're not a bad influence on Teddy—far from it—but I need to keep a close eye on him. I want him to grow up without getting into trouble. I know I have a tendency to smother him, but I can't help it. Maybe once the judge rules on permanent custody, I'll be able to relax a little." He raised an eyebrow at her, and she laughed before sobering. "Or maybe not."

"Is it because of those scars?" he asked.

"I can't help feeling that if I had been there, I might have prevented it."

"What made you comfortable enough to leave?" As soon as the words were out of his mouth, he regretted them. Although she was obviously trying to hide it, she'd been hurt by his question. Those words probably sounded more like an accusation than a simple question. Time for damage control. "Addie, I didn't mean that the way it—"

She held up a hand. "You're right. I never should have left."

He grabbed the hand she was holding up. "No. I need you to listen to me before you get it in your head that I was accusing you of anything. I'm not. You're Teddy's sister. None of what happened to him was your fault. It wasn't your responsibility to protect him. It was your mother's."

"But I knew what she could be like. I should have—"

"Didn't you say that she'd been clean for a long time?"

"She had been. At that point, anyway. I honestly don't know what happened after I left." She shook her head. "Well, I do," she muttered, bitterness lacing her tone. "She met some guy and he was a recreational user. My mother doesn't seem to understand that she's not a recreational user. Just like an alcoholic can't have just one drink. From what I can gather, he dumped her when she started using again, which only compounded the situation." She choked back a sob. "I should have stayed."

"Why? What could you have done? Honestly?"

She gave him an are-you-nuts look. "I could have prevented him from getting scalded."

"Are you saying I should have known that Tom was going to be killed that day he walked into that store?" he retorted.

"No, of course not."

He put his arm around her and held her close. "See? It doesn't mean we should stop ourselves or other people from living their lives."

"He's been wanting to walk home from the bus stop alone, and I can't quite work up to that," Addie said. "I keep thinking of all the bad things that could happen."

"Bad things happen in this world, and we can't prevent them all."

"I do the best I can to prepare him for them."

"True, but you might want to let him make some mistakes on his own," he said softly. He didn't add that it might help the boy cope in the future when the mistakes got bigger. No matter what that doctor had told him about Tracy losing the baby, he'd always wonder if he could have done something to prevent it.

She sighed. "You're right, but the thought of him walking home all alone from the bus stop..."

"Maybe we can work something out," Gabe suggested. He had an idea.

"Like what?"

"Well, I know the old lady across the street keeps a pretty keen eye out for the goings-on in our duplex. Are there any other people who could, say, be on the lookout at the time he's due to walk home?"

"There's a retired widower between here and the bus stop."

Gabe nodded. "We could check with him… Maybe he'd be willing to take a look out his window too. Would that make you feel a little more secure?"

"That might just work."

Chapter Twelve

"Do you know what kind of dates your sister likes to go on? Or if she ever has any?" Gabe asked Teddy and winced. Huh, that question had sounded a bit more subtle when he'd practiced it in his head. Not that he'd had much experience discussing dating with a seven-year-old. After setting up a tool bench in the carport, he and Teddy were working on his wooden car for the Pinewood Derby, turning the block into something that resembled a race car. He'd helped the boy make a paper pattern so they could cut the block into the shape Teddy wanted.

For the past week, Teddy had been walking home by himself from the bus stop on the days that Addie was home. When she worked, the school bus dropped him off at the library, where he did his homework, read or helped the younger kids on craft days.

Teddy scrunched up his face as he cut the paper. "Whaddaya mean dates?"

Yeah, what did he mean? He demonstrated how to put the pattern against the wood and trace. "I was just wondering if there's anything you think your sister would consider special."

"Special?" Teddy's tongue sneaked out between his lips as he concentrated on using the pencil to draw around the pattern onto the wood.

After Teddy finished tracing, Gabe clamped the wood to the table they were using. He got out safety goggles and a child-sized pair of work gloves.

Teddy looked askance at the safety items. "What's that for?"

"For you. I made sure my marines were properly equipped before sending them on a mission."

"You mean I'm like one of your marines?" the boy asked. Gabe nodded and Teddy grinned from ear to ear.

Gabe used the coping saw to get the cuts started before handing the little saw to Teddy. "Here. You take over and finish the cutting."

He helped Teddy keep the blade straight as the boy sawed through the wood. It took a while, but the block eventually turned into a wedge shape. "Now we need to sand the rough edges."

Gabe demonstrated how to rub the sandpaper over the edges.

"It sure takes lots of sanding, huh?" Teddy held up the sanded piece and turned it over in his hands. "This is really cool. Tell me again why we need to put those weight thingies in it?"

"Because a heavier car will run faster. Do you know what inertia is?"

"Uh-uh."

Gabe scratched the stubble on his cheek. "Your car needs to build up speed going downhill to sustain it along the flat part. It will eventually slow down on the flat part, but if it's going really fast, it should make it to the finish line before it stops."

"So, we can put lots of weight on it?"

Gabe shook his head. "Sorry, bud, but your car can't weigh more than five ounces total, so we'll get as close as we can without going over."

He felt frustrated at not being able to get any information out of Teddy, even though he knew it wasn't realistic or fair to be pumping the kid for it. He supposed he could approach her friend Natalie, but that sounded embarrassing.

More embarrassing than begging a child for the details of his big sister's love life?

He'd discovered Addie's birthday was coming up, and he wanted to take her on an honest-to-goodness date. What he and Addie had been doing so far on their own could be classified only as hanging out.

They'd done a lot of that lately. When Teddy was in school or off with friends, they worked more on getting her increasingly comfortable with Radar. When Teddy was there, they tossed the ball around, watched movies, ordered pizza.

As much as he enjoyed time spent with Teddy, he wanted some alone time with Addie. He wanted to explore what had started growing between them, maybe take it to the next level. Only way to accomplish that was with adult time.

"...for me, Mr. Gabe?"

Gabe glanced up from the package of decorative derby-car accessories he was attempting to open. "I'm sorry, bud—what?"

Teddy pointed to the package. "You got that 'specially for my car?"

"Sure. We want it to look cool while it's going fast."

The boy made an inarticulate sound and jumped off the stool he'd been perched on. Reaching out, he threw his arms around Gabe.

"Thank you," the boy said, his words muffled in Gabe's midsection.

Gabe blinked and swallowed against the clog in his throat. He patted Teddy on the back awkwardly. "You're entirely welcome."

Radar wandered over and whined, refusing to be left out.

The boy pulled back, surreptitiously rubbing his

nose on his sleeve. Giving the dog a hug too, Teddy giggled when Radar repaid him with sloppy kisses. He wiped his face and went back to his stool, then bent his head over his wooden car as he continued to sand it. Gabe blinked a few more times, and once the package came into focus, he finished opening the accessories. They worked in silence for a few minutes.

"Why was you asking about Addie?" Teddy asked suddenly.

"Oh, I was just wondering if anyone has taken her somewhere that she really liked. You know, it's her birthday coming up, and I thought I should know what she enjoys doing." He should be ashamed of himself, grilling Teddy about Addie's dates.

"You mean like the time she went with Mr. Ogle to that petting zoo? She said they were going to see about getting animals for the live nativity. She said that was a lot of fun, but they ended up using Brody Wilson's cow and his alpacas. I don't know if that counts."

Gabe barely restrained a chuckle. He should have realized that—

"Oh wait. I know. I know. She said she'd like someone to take her to the opera."

Opera? Attending the opera was about the last thing Gabe wanted to do. *Is this really about you? Or about giving Addie what she wants?* She'd sacrificed so much for her brother that she deserved something special for herself. "Well…if you're sure."

Teddy's head bobbed up and down. "Yup! I heard her say so herself."

"Thanks." He nodded, but his response lacked the enthusiasm of Teddy's.

After Teddy had gone home, Gabe opened up his laptop and checked. Looked like the Boston Lyric Opera was the closest to Loon Lake. He checked on dates and times. He hesitated a moment, staring at the Purchase Tickets button. Addie's sweet face appeared before him and he hit the selection. He'd survived basic training, numerous combat deployments and a bomb blast. How bad could a few hours at the opera be?

Addie made sure she oohed and aahed over Teddy's car. He and Gabe had worked on it for two days. Although the little racer was impressive, she could tell Gabe had allowed her brother to do much of the work himself. Just one more reason she was falling in love with Gabe. And she was. She might still be coming to terms with her feelings, but she couldn't deny the truth any longer.

Teddy ran to his room to put his car on his bookshelf.

"Thank you for helping him," she told Gabe.

He shrugged. "I enjoyed it as much as he did. I came back with him because I have something to ask you."

"Me?"

"I know your birthday is coming up and I wanted to do something special. Since you will soon be officially twenty-three. No more *almost* about it," he said and chuckled.

She shivered as the sexy sound made the hairs on the back of her neck stand at attention. "I've given up on the dog-years thing. So, what did you have in mind?"

He licked his lips and shifted slightly. "It, ah, would just be the two of us. If that's okay with you."

"Absolutely," she said, then felt a twinge of guilt over how quickly she'd forsaken Teddy. "I mean, I—"

"No guilt. You deserve to be spoiled a little." He reached out and cupped her cheek.

She leaned into his touch. "Thanks. Do I get a hint at what this surprise is?"

"I can tell you a little bit about it, and if you're still interested, we can finalize plans."

"O-okay." Still interested? What could he have planned? Her heart sped up. Did his plans involve taking things to the next level? Because hers did.

"It will involve going to Boston."

"I like Boston." Maybe they were on the same wavelength.

"Enough to stay overnight?" He raised an eyebrow and she nodded. "I can book a suite…separate bedrooms if…if, ah—"

"That won't be necessary." She shook her head.

His Adam's apple bobbled as he swallowed. "Okay. We can come back that night. It will be late but—"

"No, no. I meant one room is fine." Good grief. She was making a mess of this. Well, wasn't every day that a woman lost her virginity, so some nervousness was expected. Right? At least, that was the plan. "For both of us, that is."

Relief suffused his features, and he gave her a seductive lopsided grin. He leaned down and—

"Addie! Hey, Addie," Teddy called from the other room.

He touched her nose with his. "I'll go and make the hotel reservation."

"And I'll call Natalie to see if Teddy can stay with them."

"Good idea." His gaze met hers and he hesitated.

"Addie?" Teddy called again.

She watched him go and couldn't stop grinning as she went to see what Teddy wanted. She didn't know what Gabe's surprise was, but she knew how the evening would end. Even knowing she would have to confess her secret to him didn't diminish her excitement.

"Where are we going?" Addie asked for the umpteenth time after dropping Teddy off at the Gallaghers' to spend the night with Des, Natalie and Sam.

"To Boston," Gabe replied for the umpteenth time.

The stars must be in alignment because her birthday and the opera fell on the same day. Plus, she'd been granted the day off from work. A sure sign their friendship was evolving into something more.

"I know *that*, but you said later tonight was a surprise." She shifted in the passenger seat to face him. "How will I know how I'm supposed to dress if I don't know where we're going?"

He headed toward the interstate, wondering if he should have come out and told her, but the thought of surprising her had appealed to him. "You said you packed a nice dress."

"I did." She sank back into the seat. "You know you didn't have to splurge on a suite in the city. You could have booked something in one of those budget places by the highway on the outskirts."

He shrugged. Part of his reasoning had been to avoid being presumptuous. A suite with separate sleeping arrangements seemed a safer bet. He still wasn't sure if they'd be utilizing the second bedroom. Either way, he intended for this time to be special. It was about Addie, not him. "It's your birthday."

After he'd driven through town and picked up the interstate, he reached over and took her hand and interlocked their fingers.

"Thank you." She squeezed his hand. "No one has ever done anything special like this for me."

Her words reminded him of Teddy's, and he smiled, happy he could make her feel as special as she was.

Gabe negotiated the heavy Boston traffic acutely aware of the woman seated beside him. He had trouble swallowing, as if his mouth was full of sand kicked up by rotor wash in the desert.

He couldn't remember feeling this nervous about being with a woman, even in high school. Was it because ignorance had been bliss back then? Or was it because his feelings for Addie outstripped anything he'd previously felt, including those for Tracy?

He pulled into the parking garage for the hotel, glancing over at Addie before he reached for the ticket. She smiled but her lips trembled ever so slightly. Was she nervous as well?

After parking the Jeep and helping her out of the car, he shouldered their overnight bags and rested his hand on the small of her back as they headed for the elevator.

This was either going to be epic or a giant flop, he thought as he pressed the button for the lobby and the doors slid shut.

"Good afternoon," the hotel clerk greeted them as they stepped forward in the line. "Sorry for the wait."

"Looks like you're having a busy weekend," Gabe said and pulled out his wallet.

The clerk nodded. "There's a lot of people in town

for *La Bohème*. They're only doing several performances this season."

Addie nodded. "Most critics consider it his best."

Gabe handed his charge card to the desk clerk and turned to Addie. "Who?"

"Puccini."

Damn, but he was in over his head with all this opera stuff. Ask him batting averages of this year's starting lineup for the Red Sox and he'd sound knowledgeable. But this? He signed the papers the clerk handed over.

"He's the one who composed it," Addie said. "It's not just an opera but a symphony too."

Huh, maybe this was a good thing after all. He took her hand as they made their way across the lobby to the bank of elevators. "So, you really enjoy this opera stuff?"

She shrugged. "I've never been. Never gave much thought to it. Why?"

"But you enjoy listening to it?" he asked as they stepped into the elevator.

"Can't say that I do."

The elevator doors slid shut, and he narrowed his eyes, suspicion thumping in his chest. Why had Teddy told him this was what she'd wanted more than anything for her birthday? Had he been had by Teddy, or had the boy made an honest mistake?

"You seemed to know a lot about this Puccini guy."

Grinning, she tucked her hand around his arm. "Haven't you learned by now that I know a little bit about a lot of things?"

The elevator glided to a stop and the doors opened. "Are you saying you're *not* into opera?"

"Sorry to disappoint you, but the only opera I knew before was from watching an old *Seinfeld* episode." She squeezed his arm before letting go. "Is this my surprise? Are you a closet opera fan?"

He inserted the key card into the lock. The electronic mechanism whirred and clicked. He pushed open the door and indicated for her to go before him.

"What a gorgeous room," she said and twirled around, arms held wide.

"About this opera thing…" He shut the door and set their bags down. May as well come clean. "I've already bought tickets."

She dropped her arms and went to him. "I admit I am surprised by your choice. I'd have figured you more for baseball and hot dogs. But it'll be great."

Yeah, great. What he wouldn't give for the crack of a bat and a cold beer. He groaned and rubbed a hand over his face. Served him right for taking dating advice from a seven-year-old.

"Teddy," he muttered sotto voce.

She tilted her head. "What's he got to do with all this?"

"He's the reason we have opera tickets." He sighed. "I asked for his advice, and that is what he suggested."

She burst out laughing. "I'm sorry, but—"

"Yeah." He nodded.

She threw her arms around him. "This is the best thing anyone has done for me. I feel like Cinderella."

His arms held her close when she would have pulled back. "But—"

She cut off his protests with her lips on his.

"Best birthday ever," she said against his lips.

Not about to let a chance to kiss Addie pass him by, he pressed his lips to hers and coaxed her mouth open. Their tongues dueled and sent his pulse surging through his veins.

He hated to pull away, but blood was starting to leave his brain and he wanted her to enjoy every bit of the evening before things got out of hand.

"I made dinner reservations at an Italian restaurant nearby," he told her and rested his forehead against hers.

"Then I'd better get dressed." She started for one of the bedrooms but turned before entering. "I thought you were going to get us a regular room."

He shrugged. "They were booked up, so I kept the suite."

Dimples scored her cheeks. "Okay. Just checking."

That smile made him weak in the knees.

Later that evening when he was sitting listening to music he didn't understand in shoes that pinched, he thought about that kiss and how the evening would end.

He reached for Addie's hand. Maybe Teddy's advice wasn't such a disaster after all. Making a mental note to tell her again how beautiful she looked tonight, he squeezed her hand and she turned to him and smiled.

Although she'd enjoyed her very first opera, during the stirring performances, Addie's thoughts kept straying to how this evening might end. He'd kept the suite, but she didn't think there'd be a need for the second bedroom.

The entire evening was overshadowed by what would be coming at the end of it. At least, she hoped it was coming. Should she tell Gabe? If he changed his mind, then what?

Stop being such a drama queen, she cautioned herself. People didn't actually die of embarrassment.

If she didn't tell him, would he be able to figure it out? Were normal guys—not those larger-than-life heroes in books—able to tell?

What was she even thinking? Of course she had to tell him.

And now that they were making their way back to the hotel, one thought kept racing through her mind. *Tell him.* That insistent voice in her head wouldn't be quieted.

But all her good intentions vanished when they

entered the common area of their suite and he shut the door, reaching for her.

He brought his mouth down on hers, and she opened immediately for him, her tongue meeting his. Without lifting his mouth from hers, he began walking her backward to the bedroom he'd used to get ready.

Once there, he frowned at her dress. "How does this work?"

Feeling giddy from his kisses, she giggled. "It's a wraparound. See?"

She undid the garment and let it fall open, then tossed it onto a chair by the bed with much more bravado than she was feeling. Maybe fake-it-till-you-make-it wasn't such a good idea here.

"Mmm, very user-friendly," he said, his eyes widening.

"You can thank Diane von Furstenberg." She waved her hand. "Don't ask."

"Okay." He laughed, shucked his jacket and toed off his leather dress shoes with a deep sigh.

"What?"

"Those pinched," he said and undid his belt.

Oh dear, things were progressing at a faster pace than she'd anticipated. She really needed to confess.

He pulled down his pants while unbuttoning his shirt. He tossed aside the shirt and removed his socks. Clothed in nothing but navy blue boxer briefs, he took her into his arms.

She could feel how ready he was. Physically she was because her panties were soaked from just watching his haste to undress. But the fact she was still thinking about it made her wonder if she was mentally ready. "You're wearing the pink lace bra," he groaned. "I have been having dreams about it."

They fell silent for several minutes as they explored one another's bodies. Addie reveled in being able to run her hands over his impressive chest. She lightly traced several angry-looking scars, her heart aching for him.

She looked up at him. "The blast?"

He nodded, and when he opened his mouth, she put her fingers over it and began kissing each scar.

Groaning, he laid her on the bed. "My turn," he whispered and removed her bra. He sucked on one nipple, then the other. He slowly worked his way down her stomach and circled her belly button with his tongue. His fingers dipped under the waistband of her lace thong, and she shivered with unexpected sensation. But she jerked her head up and out of the delicious delirium…

"Gabe…"

He lifted his head, his pupils flared and dilated. "What is it?"

"There's, uh, something I should probably tell you."

He scooted up so his gaze was even with hers.

When he frowned, she drew in a deep breath, fear coiling in her gut. "I've never...you know..."

She motioned her hand back and forth between them. Talk about embarrassing. She shouldn't have even brought it up. Would he have been able to tell? Did guys even notice those things? It wasn't as if this were one of those Victorian romances where women knew next to nothing. She understood the difference between fantasy and real life. And considering her age, she was a virgin because she'd never had sex, but it had nothing to do with a certain belief. She'd been ready years ago. She'd wanted her first time to be with someone special, and that special someone hadn't come until now.

"Uh, Addie?" he interrupted her musings. "Could you be a little more specific?"

Her face on fire as much from what she'd been thinking as from the situation, she blew out her breath. "I haven't...had sex before. Ever."

He sat up. "You're telling me that you're a virgin?" Shock was written all over his features, and she cringed.

"Yeah. That."

"But you're twenty-three."

"That's why it's a bit embarrassing," she admitted.

"I knew you were too young for me," he muttered and swung his legs over the side of the bed. *No!*

"Now, hold on." She grabbed his arm. "Are you saying you've changed your mind? Is that what's going on here? And how the hell am I too young for you? How do you figure that? I'm twenty-three, no more *almost* about it, and you're thirty. Seven years is nothing."

"I was thinking more in terms of—"

"No," she interrupted, swatting his arm. She knew where this was going and wasn't going to let him get away with it. "You don't get to pull that life-experiences card. I'm sure you suffered a lot of horrific, life-changing things in Afghanistan, but my childhood was not all about Mom, apple pie and family togetherness."

"You're right about your experiences being different from mine, but—" He pressed a finger over her mouth when she opened it. "Let me finish. Yes, I was going to say different, but no less traumatic."

"Okay, but I'm confused. If you agree I'm not some clueless kid, does that mean you want to continue?"

"I definitely want to continue." His gaze met hers, and he made what sounded like a groan deep in his throat. "But I have to be sure. This is a big step for you...bigger than I had imagined when I planned this."

"Well, I need to get rid of my status at some point," she muttered. "I certainly don't want to die a...virgin."

He raised an eyebrow. "Are librarians allowed

to use that sort of language? Not to mention all the money you'll be owing the swear jar."

She frowned. "You mean *virgin*?"

"I was referring to that verb you were *thinking* of using as an adjective."

She shook her head. How did...? "But I didn't say it out loud."

His sudden, deep-throated chuckle sent tingles down her spine, and she shivered.

"You didn't have to say the word. It was on your face." He placed his fingertip on her cheek and lightly traced the freckles.

"Don't you want to," she joked, changing the pitch of her voice, "boldly go where no man has gone before?" She wanted him badly, but she wasn't sure how to proceed. It wasn't as if she'd done any of this before.

He burst out laughing. "I'm not sure about the *boldly* part." He frowned. "But you do know your status has nothing to do with how I feel about you and this, right? Whether or not you were a virgin, I'd still want to be with you. I care about you."

"I would hope so."

"You're special, no matter what," he said and lowered his head.

Taking his time, he used his tongue all over her body, licking and teasing parts she had no idea were so erogenous. Who knew the backs of her knees were so sensitive? Or that spot where her neck met her shoulder? His tongue was magic, and he knew how to use it.

"Gabe," she begged. Was that hoarse whisper hers?

"Tell me what you want."

"I don't know what..." She squirmed. "...to ask for."

Evidently he knew, because his fingers found that spot that craved his touch. "Is this it?"

"Yes. Please." She wasn't above begging. "Gabe..."

"Let it happen, Addie."

And she did. She understood the reference to fireworks in those books.

He removed his boxer briefs and scooted up. "Are you ready for me?"

"Yes."

He reached over her to the bedside table and grabbed the condom he'd left there earlier. "These are pre-lubricated, but I don't think we need it. Still, I don't want to hurt you."

"This is the twenty-first century. I know to expect some discomfort the first time."

He rolled the condom on and slowly entered, filling her, but then stopped. Was something wrong? Why had he stopped? Despite the discomfort, she liked the fact he was filling her. She knew physically the act would be similar with someone else, but the fact it was Gabe stretching her made her heart do a little flip-flop.

"Uh, Gabe? I know this is my first time and all, but aren't you supposed to be moving or something?" Why was she expecting him to do it all? "Is it my fault? Am I supposed…? I mean, am I not…?"

"It's me." He groaned. "If I don't do box scores in my head to slow this down, it's gonna be over soon."

"Oh. But that's okay. We've got all night. I mean, in all those books—"

He made a noise that was a cross between a groan and a laugh. "Exactly what books have you been reading?"

"The good ones?"

He laughed and started to move. It ached a bit at first, but then delightful sensations soon began to rocket through her body. "Tell me if anything hurts."

"Want me to raise my left hand like at the dentist?" she gasped. "Sorry—am I killing the mood?"

He grabbed her left hand and brought it to his lips and kissed her palm. "What happens here is between us, and we can be any way we want."

"Was that a yes or a no to raising my hand?" she teased.

"You tell me to stop and I will."

"Oh no. Please don't stop now that it's getting good."

He lifted up on his elbow to look into her eyes. "Just getting good?"

She smiled dreamily. "It was all good before… very good…excellent."

"And now?"

She ran her fingers through his hair. "What's better than excellent? Transcendental?"

He hooted a laugh.

"Don't stop. I'll keep quiet."

"But, sweetness, if you're quiet, how will I know if I'm being transcendental or not?"

She lifted up and kissed him.

He used his finger to bring her to the brink again and waited until she'd tumbled over before he thrust one last time and cried out her name.

Chapter Thirteen

Afterward, he pulled her into his arms and brushed the hair back from her face. He'd done his best to make it as good for her as it had been for him. But he also knew that was impossible, because no matter how gentle he'd been, she'd experienced discomfort.

She'd thrown him for a loop when she'd admitted this was her first time. He'd been scared but concentrated on making it good for her. In doing so, he'd made it ground shaking for him. For the first time, he'd not only experienced physical satisfaction, but the tenderness of the moment shifted something inside him. So, in essence, it was a first for him too.

An idea occurred to him and he got out of bed. "Be right back. Stay there."

She laughed. "I have no plans to go anywhere."

In the bathroom, he ran warm water onto a wash-cloth. Back in the bedroom, he showed it to her and gently ran it over her body, kissing and caressing as he went. "This may help if you have some discomfort."

He threw it into the sink after they were done. Crawling back into bed with her, he pulled the covers over them and held her. "Sorry if my surprise was a bit off the mark."

She rubbed her cheek against his chest as she curled into him. "Considering I had a surprise for you too, it's okay. I actually enjoyed it. What about you?"

"Oh, I *definitely* enjoyed it."

She lifted her head to look at his face. "You may well turn into an opera buff."

"Oh. You were talking about the opera."

She laughed and he kissed her nose. A feeling that defied description rose in his chest. He didn't know what to do with all the tender feelings rising up. It was like when Teddy had thrown his arms around him but even more indescribable.

She threw one of her legs over his. "Tell me about your dad. You mentioned a few things but not much. I overheard what Ogle said about him at the meeting."

He kissed the top of her head. "I forgot to thank you for making me go."

She lifted her head. "I did not *make* you go."

He chuckled. "Ah, but you did, because it was either show up or have you disappointed in me."

"Really?"

"Yup. But I'm glad you invited me. Ogle told me things I didn't know about Pa, things I wouldn't have realized on my own."

"What do you mean? You must've known your dad was pretty special."

He wasn't proud of his feelings from back then, but he wanted her to know him, even if it meant telling her things he'd have preferred not to. She meant too much to him now. "I wasn't a very good son."

"I don't believe that for one minute."

"It's true. I was ashamed of where we lived. All that junk in the front yard and the fact he always had low-paying jobs. What kind of son did that make me?"

"A normal kid. Want to talk about being ashamed...? My mother was an addict who exchanged sex for drugs. As for you and your father, I would say you were embarrassed. I think there's a big difference between that and being ashamed. You said he did the best he could after your mom died, and I heard the caring in your voice and saw it in your eyes."

"I disappointed him." He shook his head, flooded with memories. "His greatest wish for me was to go to college so I could do better than him. Instead, I got a girl pregnant, had to get married and joined the marines. Never made it to college."

"Well, no matter what you say, I heard Ogle saying how proud your dad was. Quit blaming yourself for acting like a teenager when you were eighteen."

"Maybe you should take your own advice," he told her.

"What's that supposed to mean?"

"It means you should quit blaming yourself for what happened to Teddy. If anyone was at fault, and I'm still not sure about that, it would be your mother."

"But if I had been there—"

"Don't." He took both her hands in his and squeezed. "You were a kid yourself."

She made noises with her tongue on the roof of her mouth. "I was eighteen."

"Exactly."

"You were in the marines, taking responsibility, when you were eighteen."

"Actually, I was nineteen when I joined the Corps."

"Because you wanted to provide for yourself and your wife."

He snorted, unable to give himself a break, even if he'd been confronting someone else in the same situation. He'd said they needed to cut themselves some slack. Teenagers often acted their age. "More like running away."

"How is joining the marines running away?"

How often had he run away from those feelings gripping him, threatening to overwhelm him? The fact they'd lost their son—even one he hadn't gotten to know—rubbed him so raw he'd suppressed it, fed himself platitudes.

"Losing the baby changed everything. Tracy changed… I changed. I was sorry about the late-stage miscarriage, but deep down I'm ashamed to admit I was probably relieved. God—" he ran a hand over his scalp "—isn't that a terrible thing to admit?"

"You were both young and tried to do the right thing." She shook her head. "Maybe everything would have worked out. You have no way of knowing and shouldn't beat yourself up over being young."

"So should you. Why is my situation any different than yours?" he shot back.

"Maybe you're right." She heaved a deep sigh. "But I can't believe she divorced you while you were serving your country."

He knew the town had been outraged on his behalf. To his great shame, he'd done nothing to change that. Maybe it was time he did. "That's not totally accurate."

"Oh?"

"History has been known to get rewritten by the folks in Loon Lake."

"Like that children's game of telephone."

He nodded. "Exactly. I came home before deployment, and we pretty much called it quits, so the divorce proceedings were just a formality. Neither of us was happy, and we'd gotten married only for the baby's sake."

"She still shouldn't have done that, in my opinion."

"Don't make me out to be the injured party here. I'm the one who took the coward's way out and left when things got tough."

"Joining the marines for a better future wasn't cowardly. You said yourself how hard it was getting steady employment once the economy took a downturn. You were doing what had to be done to secure a better future."

"I literally abandoned her," he said bluntly. "There's no way to sugarcoat that."

"I hate to say this, but a lot of marriages falter after the death of a child."

"That may be true, but I didn't put enough work into it. Just like playing baseball or going to college, like my pa wanted."

"How old were you when you got married?"

"I had just turned eighteen." He shook his head. "Barely out of high school."

"You did the honorable thing by her. You didn't have to."

"Of course I had to. She was pregnant and... scared."

"Loon Lake might be small-town, but it wasn't the 1950s."

"What're you saying?"

"That I think you acted honorably. And you each moved on when you realized there was nothing left for you in your marriage. Now you're free to be happy."

She snuggled closer, and pretty soon her breathing had evened out. He lay awake wishing he could be different, be the kind of guy who stuck. For her. And for the kid. But could he ever be the man she wanted him to be?

The next morning, he shifted, trying to ease away from her, but he ended up waking her.

"Sorry about that," he muttered. "You can ignore it."

She laughed. "I thought all guys had a morning—"

He put a finger over her mouth. "This is an Addie one. Not simply a morning one."

She blushed and grinned. "That's nice to know. Are you planning on doing something about it?"

"I thought you might be too sore."

"It's okay," she told him. "Do you have another condom?"

"I may not have been a Cub Scout like Teddy, but I am prepared."

"That's good to know," she said and turned toward him.

Oh God, how he loved this woman, he thought as he pulled her into his arms. His heart began to pound as he realized what he'd just admitted to himself. For a moment he froze, letting that knowledge sink in.

"Gabe? Something wrong?"

He looked into her eyes, saw the worry in them and kissed her forehead.

"No. Nothing's wrong. For once, everything is right." And he set about showing just how right things were with her.

Gabe was turning onto his street when his phone dinged, indicating a text. He pulled into his driveway and checked the message. It was from Addie, asking him to come ASAP. He frowned. It had been two weeks since their trip to Boston. Despite his fear of letting her down, things had seemed to be going well. They'd been spending all their free time together, doing family things like watching movies on school nights and mini golf on the weekend. He'd even managed to help Teddy with his homework a few times.

The more times they were together, the more he believed he could be in it for the long haul. When he thought about the future, he thought in terms of Addie and Teddy.

With Addie's encouragement, he began studying for his contractor's license.

After parking his Jeep, he didn't even bother to go to his place but let himself into her place. "Addie? What's going on? I got your text."

"In here."

He followed the sound of her voice into the kitchen.

She stood by the sink. "I'm so glad you're here."

She looked and sounded relieved to see him, filling him with pride. He went to her and took her into his arms. He patted her back when she sagged against him. "What's wrong? Are you okay?"

She nodded and pulled away. "I just had a bit of a fright."

He wanted to take her back into his embrace. She felt so good, like she belonged, but she backed away. "Tell me."

She took a deep breath. "There's a snake on the step leading to the carport."

"What?" He started to get a queasy feeling in his stomach. He hated snakes. Yeah, a walking Indiana Jones cliché. He'd heard it all before and therefore did his best to keep it hidden. Huh, a lot like Addie with her cynophobia.

"I couldn't find my wallet, and I was going out to see if I'd left it in the car. I opened the door and glanced down, and there it was. Just curled up on the step."

He shrugged. "Sounds to me as if it was simply minding its own business. Not hurting anyone."

"Yeah, well, it can mind its business elsewhere."

"So, you want me to kill a snake because it innocently wandered into your carport?"

"Absolutely not! I don't even like killing bugs. I always feel so guilty after." She stuck out her bottom lip in a pout.

"After?" He had the urge to take that bottom lip between his teeth. *Go for it*, his inner voice urged. Create a distraction and maybe the stupid thing would slither away. Problem solved. "So, you do kill bugs."

"This isn't about whether or not I kill bugs. I'm asking you to deal with the snake."

"Want me to call it an Uber and send it over to Montpelier? Is that far enough away?"

"Go ahead. Make fun."

"You're asking me to risk my life for a snake?"

"Vermont doesn't have venomous snakes… Well, unless you count the handful of timber rattlesnakes over in Rutland County."

"What?" He blinked. "You mean there are poisonous snakes in Vermont?"

"Like I said, there are over in Rut—"

"And I suppose you're going to tell me they respect borders?"

She narrowed her eyes at him, and the speculative glance she gave him had him shifting his weight from one leg to the other.

"Do you have a thing about snakes?" she asked.

He shook his head, unwilling to hand over his

man card that easily. "No. I just think they should be allowed their freedom."

"And I agree, as long as it's not anywhere near me." She glared at him, but her eyes contained a mischievous glint. "Ophidiophobia."

He wet his lips and repeated the word. "Hmm. Sounds interesting… What is it?"

She made a noise with her tongue, but a grin lifted her lips. "That's what the fear of snakes is called."

He huffed out a breath. "I am not afraid. It's just a healthy respect."

"Of course," she said and nodded. "Just like I had a healthy respect for dogs."

"That's different," he scoffed, but he returned her grin. His pride wasn't such that he was insulted. Besides, even if he was, she was too cute for him to stay annoyed.

"Oh? How is that different?"

"Snakes don't have fur and big brown eyes."

"Maybe this one does." She pointed to the door. "You should go check it out."

"I'd rather check out something I've been thinking about since your wet T-shirt show."

He leaned forward and brought his lips closer to hers. She parted her lips in anticipation of—

"Addie? Can I—? Whoa." Teddy skidded to a stop in the doorway to the kitchen. "What're you guys doing?"

Gabe closed his eyes and rubbed the back of his neck. Talk about embarrassing. He and Addie had briefly discussed what they were going to tell Teddy about their relationship but hadn't done it yet. Looked like they'd run out of time, but he'd follow her lead.

Addie jumped back and tugged on the front of her shirt. "We—" She cleared her throat. "We were discussing Gabe's fear of—"

"I'm not afraid of—"

"Mr. Gabe ain't afraid of nothing!" Teddy stuck out his chin.

"Gabe's not afraid of *anything*," Addie said.

Teddy looked confused. "That's what I said."

"Gee, it's a relief to see we're in agreement over my lack of fear of snakes." He wasn't above smirking at her.

"I wasn't referring to your fears but correcting Teddy's double negative." Addie narrowed her eyes at him.

"What's a double negative?" Teddy demanded.

"It means you said Gabe wasn't afraid twice in the same sentence."

"Well, the kid knows what he's saying." He'd been trying to lighten the mood, but, judging from her expression, his technique needed work.

"Teddy, your two negatives turn it into a positive."

"Huh?" Teddy scrunched up his face.

"It means he is afraid of snakes."

"Why is it okay for you to be afraid of dogs but not for me to feel the same about snakes?"

The only sound in the room was Teddy's shocked gasp.

Addie's stomach dropped below her knees. She was sure Gabe had been teasing. Nevertheless, she shot him a quelling glance. But she was afraid to look at her brother for fear he'd see the truth written on her features.

"Addie? Is it true?"

"Teddy, look, I can ex—"

"No!" Teddy shouted. "You lied to me. You said dogs were expensive, but that's a lie. You just don't want me to have one. I don't want to live here anymore. Mom says I can have a dog if I go live with her." He turned and ran out of the room.

A door slamming reverberated through the house. Torn between running after him and letting Teddy cool off, she turned helplessly in a circle.

A hand came to rest on her shoulder, halting her and guiding her toward a chair. Gabe pulled it out with his foot. "Give him a few minutes to cool off."

She sank onto the seat. "I should have been honest with him from the beginning."

She pressed her fist against her mouth. He hunkered down in front of her and pulled her hand away and held it in his.

"I f—messed up, and I'm sorry," Gabe murmured. "Do you want me to talk to him?"

"No. That's my responsibility. I should have taken your advice sooner and been totally honest with him about everything." She sighed and got up. "I'd better go speak with him."

"Want some help?"

She shook her head. "It's my responsibility. I'm his guardian. I'll handle it."

"I'm going to go let Radar out. He's been cooped up all day."

She nodded and went into Teddy's room. She knocked but didn't wait for a response that might never come.

He was lying on his bed, his face in a pillow.

She sat on the bed and touched his back. "I'm sorry. It was wrong to mislead you. I know that now. I'm not wrong about how expensive dogs can be, but I should have explained about my fear. I hope you will still want to live with me. Once I finish my college degree, I might be able to get a job as head librarian and we can see about affording a dog. But I can't make any promises." She patted his back and smoothed a hand over his hair. "I am sorry and I hope you'll forgive me." No response whatsoever.

She sighed and got up to leave. She made it into the hall and was going to close his door.

"Addie?" He turned over.

Addie's heart ached when she saw his face. She

could tell he'd been crying. She'd been too afraid to give in to tears because once they started, she might not be able to stop them. "What is it, Teddy?"

"I'm sorry. I didn't mean it when I said I didn't want to live with you." He sniffed and sat up. "Please don't hate me."

She stepped back into the room and he sprang off the bed.

"Oh, Teddy, c'mere. I love you. I could never hate you, no matter what you said." She opened her arms and he ran into them. They clung to one another. Taking comfort from each other.

Teddy lifted his head. "Even if Mom gets better, I want to stay here. Please don't send me away."

"I would never do that. I promise."

"I was just a stupid kid when I got burned. I wouldn't do anything like that again. I promise. Please don't send me away."

"You can be with me forever, sweetie. That's why we have to go to court."

He gazed up at her, searching her face. "Is it still okay to love her? Even if I don't want to live with her?"

"Of course it is, sweetie. She's our mother." She blinked back tears. She'd struggled with some of the same things. Gabe had been right. They should have been honest and talked things out. "You know our mom isn't a bad person."

He shrugged. "Everyone said she's sick."

"In a way, I guess she is. She has a drug problem. Do you know what that means?"

"A policeman comes and tells us about that stuff in school." He nodded and sniffed. "You would never do that, right?"

"No, I wouldn't, but I also shouldn't have lied to you. It's just that when I was your age, I was bitten by a dog. I know you love dogs and probably can't understand that I was afraid of them."

He touched her hand. "I'll bet it's like how I didn't want to take a bath after I got burned. I was afraid to touch the water in case I got burned again."

"I guess you do understand. I'm sorry I wasn't there to help you, Teddy. But I'm working through my fear, thanks to Gabe and Radar. Just like you did with the hot water. We're both brave, right?"

"Yeah. And the social worker lady kept telling me you were too young to take care of me, but I said that wasn't true and that you would never act like Mom. And that's what I'm going to tell them when we go to talk to that judge person."

She hoped so. Because now she couldn't imagine her life without Teddy—or Gabe—in it.

Chapter Fourteen

Addie paced the living room waiting for Teddy. She'd agreed to Gabe's plan to let Teddy walk home from the bus stop alone that afternoon. Usually, on the days she was working, he took the bus that dropped him off at the library, where he did his homework, read or helped with the younger kids doing crafts.

She spotted him coming down the sidewalk, but this wasn't his normal gait. Something was wrong. She just knew it.

She flung the door open and ran down the steps. He wasn't wearing his glasses, and his shirt was ripped. He looked as if he'd been in a fight.

"Oh my God, Teddy, what happened to you?" As if she didn't already know. She rubbed her hands up and down her arms, hoping to get the blood flowing. She felt as if she'd never feel warm again. How could she have let this happen?

She hunkered down in front of him. His eye was an angry red and violet, the edges already starting to turn yellow. "Oh, Teddy, look at your eye."

He shook his head. "Addie, you know I can't see it without a mirror."

He has the beginnings of a black eye. She closed her own. This couldn't be happening. And on the day before their court appearance. She would be standing before a judge with Teddy sporting a giant bruise on his face.

"I'm sorry, Addie." His face crumpled. He held out his twisted glasses in the flat of his palm.

"There, there. Glasses can be replaced." She pulled him close for a hug. She was just glad he was all right.

He sniffed. "I should have taken them off like Mr. Gabe said."

"What do you mean, like Mr. Gabe said?"

"He was showing me some…some defensive moves and said to always remove my glasses so they don't get broke."

Gabe had been showing Teddy how to fight? When the judge asked how he got the black eye, would he tell them that his sister's friend was teaching him to fight? She'd be labeled as a negligent parent, just like their mother. Teddy was in her care; he was her responsibility, not Gabe's. How dare Gabe do this to her? He knew the hearing was tomorrow. He knew how tenuous her situation was.

She groaned. This was all her fault. She should've taken better care of Teddy, listened to her instincts, not let someone else influence her.

"Here he comes now."

Sure enough, the Jeep was pulling into the driveway.

"Teddy, go in the house," she said shortly. "I'll be in, and we'll put some ice on your eye." See if they could mitigate the damage.

"But I want to show Mr. Gabe my—"

"Not now. Go inside," she said, doing her best to keep her tone even.

"But, Addie—"

"Now, Teddy."

He muttered something about fairness, twirled around and stomped into the house.

A car door slammed and she drew in a deep breath, barely able to control her fury. Who did he think he was? He'd gone behind her back and betrayed her. Served her right for ever getting involved in the first place. She'd had misgivings in the beginning. Why had she allowed herself to get sucked in? She was no better than their mother, letting a man come before her duty to Teddy.

"What's going on?" Gabe strolled across the lawn toward her. "Is Teddy okay?"

"No, he's not. He came home with a black eye and busted glasses." She shook her head, striving for calm but not achieving it.

"Is he hurt?"

"It's nothing permanent." She shook her head. "I knew letting him walk home alone was a mistake. The school didn't contact me, so I can only assume this happened at the bus stop."

"Did you ask him?"

No, she hadn't. Not really. Which made her the most irresponsible parent ever. Her one job was to keep Teddy safe and she'd failed.

"Not yet," she admitted.

"Boys get into scrapes." He put a hand on her shoulder, but she brushed it off.

She didn't deserve to be comforted. She'd brought all this on by being lax with Teddy—and letting a man she barely knew take on a paternal role with her brother. *Her* brother, her responsibility. Not his. "Is that what you did? I know you're the big war hero now, but it seems like everyone has a story to tell about the things you did as a teen. Are you trying to turn my brother into a delinquent like you?"

Oh God, Addie, what are you doing, lashing out?

She held up her hand. "Look, I didn't—" But the damage had already been done; Gabe looked stunned and hurt. It was as if the connection between them had been severed by a sharp knife.

He held up his hands, palms out. "You're right. I'm a lousy role model for a kid."

"No. Honest, I didn't mean it." She hated the pleading note in her voice but couldn't help it.

He shook his head. "No, you're right. We should both go inside before we say something we might regret."

Too late. "Yeah, I should go check on Teddy."

He shoved his hands in his pockets. "Tell Teddy I hope he's okay. And don't worry—I'll stay away from him from now on. From both of you."

"If you want…" Tears pricked at her eyes. She couldn't imagine losing Gabe now, but she had to do what was best for her brother. She hadn't meant…

He shook his head. "I'm going inside, Addie. You should too."

She nodded and watched him walk away. He went into his home without a backward glance. She stood motionless for a moment, staring at his closed door. Her world had just ended…not with a bang, but with the closing of a door. She felt dizzy, sick to her stomach. Would she ever be whole again? Not having Gabe in her life would be like not having Teddy.

Teddy. She needed to check on him, get some ice on his eye.

He was in his room, sitting on the end of the bed, staring at his glasses in his lap. She joined him and sat next to him. Picking up his glasses, she said, "I'll see if we can salvage these until we can get new ones."

"I'm sorry, Addie."

She put her arm around him, hiding her face in his hair so he wouldn't see her eyes brimming with tears. "I know you are. Want to tell me why you got into a fight?"

"That new kid, Brandon, was making fun of Sam because he can't talk. I tol' him that not being able to say stuff without his tablet didn't make him dumb. But he kept saying it did, so when we got off the bus I tol' him to take it back, and when he wouldn't, I punched him in the stomach."

She winced but resisted scolding. "Then what happened?"

"He's bigger'n me and he punched me back. I was gonna still fight him, but he ran away."

She sighed and hugged her brother. "You know I don't condone fighting—for any reason."

"I know, but..." He shrugged.

"But I am proud of you for standing up for Sam. You are a good friend."

"I like Sam."

"So do I." She squeezed him and kissed the top of his head before standing up. "We'll put some ice on that eye. Maybe it won't look so bad tomorrow."

"What if it does?"

"All you can do is tell the truth." She squared her

shoulders. And that was all she could do too—to Gabe, to herself and to the judge. Even if that meant she lost the man she realized she loved...forever.

After ministering to Teddy's eye and leaving him eating ice cream at the table, she straightened her spine and walked the few steps to Gabe's place.

She knocked on the door and tried to gather her thoughts. How could she make this right? What if she'd hurt him beyond repair?

"Hey," he said when he opened the door. "How's Teddy?"

"Nothing wrong that a bowl of ice cream and some Gorilla Glue can't fix," she said, shifting her weight from one foot to the other.

"Glue?" His tone lacked inflection. His face was as blank as his voice, his body held rigidly straight.

She managed a wobbly smile. "For his glasses."

Radar came over and sat next to Gabe in the doorway. Steadying her nerves, she reached out to pet him on the head. "He's probably looking for Teddy."

Gabe grunted in reply and looked away, refusing to make eye contact.

Okay, well, this might take a bit more than a simple apology. "I shouldn't have lashed out at you like that. I was wrong and I want you to know that."

He shrugged, reminding her of Teddy when he was trying to pretend his feelings weren't hurt. She should have thought before she said anything. Too late now.

"I shouldn't have interfered," he said.

"Teddy's skirmish had nothing to do with him walking alone from the bus stop. I was wrong not giving him some responsibility. He was fighting because a kid was picking on Sam Gallagher."

"The one who is nonverbal?"

"Yeah. Teddy was sticking up for him. I can't blame him for that. And it isn't your fault either. I shouldn't have said what I did. I was angry, but not at you—at myself. I didn't have any right to say those things."

"People sometimes say how they honestly feel when they're angry."

She shook her head vehemently, trying to make him see that she'd just been worried for her brother. "No. This was bound to happen. Maybe it's better to have happened at the end of the street. Teddy might have gotten himself suspended if he'd fought at school. And you're not a bad role model, Gabe. Far from it, in fact."

He rubbed the back of his neck. "What about tomorrow's hearing?"

"There's not much I can do about it except tell the truth and pray. Like you say, boys get into scrapes, and I have to trust that the judge will understand."

"He might not have, if I hadn't encouraged him." He raised his hands, palms out, in front of him. "I'm not a good candidate to be a father figure to a seven-year-old boy. I can't get my own sh—stuff together. How am I supposed to set an example? I can't even stop swearing."

"My brother doesn't need some saint or war hero. Maybe he just needs someone to look up to who's good and kind and decent. It doesn't matter if you make mistakes. God knows I've made plenty."

"It's not just—"

"Except it is! That's exactly what it is."

He shook his head. "I'm not following you."

"Teddy needs to know that someone will be there for him…day in and day out. Someone who won't disappear for hours and leave him to fend for himself. Like our mom," she added bitterly.

Gabe took a step back. "Is that what happened?"

"He won't talk about it. But it's what happened to me, so I have to assume she left him on his own a whole lot too." She wiped her face with the back of her hand, which she waved around. "Look, I see why you don't want to get involved. We're a package deal, me and Teddy, and we come with a lot of baggage."

He ran his fingers through his hair. "I'm the one who is messed up. I already have one failed marriage. I don't want another."

She raised an eyebrow. "Oh, has there been a proposal? Did I miss that?"

"You know what I mean." A muscle ticked in his cheek.

"You were a kid when you got married. How can you blame yourself for that?"

"If things were so great, why did she divorce me?"

It was like talking to a brick wall, but she had to try. "I don't know. Did you ask her?"

"I just signed the papers when she sent them."

"And you're the one preaching to me about talking with Teddy…being open and honest. And you couldn't even confront your own wife?" The words had left her mouth before her brain could catch up. He made her react in ways she couldn't control.

"You're right. I have no right to offer any advice to you or your brother. That's why this won't work. I'm the last person you should be listening to."

Desperation clawed at her chest. She hadn't felt this helpless since that dog had clamped his jaws around her. She laid her hand on his arm. "But don't you see? That's why you're perfect for us. You're offering guidance you've learned from experience. I didn't have a chance to tell you, but I took your advice and was honest with Teddy. I told him that I didn't want to alienate him from Michelle but that I also didn't trust her."

"He doesn't trust her either."

"Did he tell you that?"

He nodded. "I didn't want to break my promise

to him not to tell, but I couldn't let you two go on at cross-purposes."

"And I can't tell you how grateful I am."

"At least something good came out of this."

Her heart began to pound as his words sank in. "What do you mean? You're making this sound like it's the end of something."

"Something that never should have started. I knew better than to get involved with someone like you."

Confusion flooded her mind. "What do you mean, someone like *me*?"

"Someone who expects…expects…" Gabe waved his hands in the air.

"Expects what?" She had an ominous feeling about this. She wanted to cover her ears, block out what he was about to say, but she couldn't do that. She was done with running from the truth—now and forever, whether it was about her family or why she'd feared dogs for so long. And if Gabe didn't want to be with her, even after all they'd shared—well, she'd just have to deal with that too. Just like she'd dealt with everything else in her life.

"Happily-ever-after," he said, sounding as if the concept left a bad taste in his mouth. "I don't do *forever*… Ask my ex. Ask the Corps. Things get tough and I bail."

"I never asked you for happily-ever-after." But

she could admit to herself she wanted it. How she longed for it—with him.

"But you expected it."

"No, what I expected was just *ever after*. I can make my own happiness." She swallowed past the clog in her throat and blinked. "You can choose to be a part of it or not."

"I guess I choose not."

She started to leave but turned back. "I'll try to explain it to Teddy. He'll be devastated." She inhaled and struggled to get the next words out. "But you know what they say—kids are resilient, so don't worry about us."

Gabe stood in the middle of the room after she'd left, fighting the urge to go after her.

Why? So he could mess up her life too?

A cold wet nose shoved into his palm. Radar made a new noise. A sort of grumble. "What're you? My conscience?"

Radar whined and Gabe shook his head. "It's for the best."

So why did doing the right thing have to hurt so damn much? Like a big black hole had opened in his chest, sucking up all the oxygen and making it hard to breathe. He staggered to the couch and threw himself down. Slumping over, he rested his elbows on his knees and held his head in his hands.

Are you trying to turn my brother into a delinquent like you?

Addie's words echoed in his head and he groaned. The truth hurt. He shook his head. No, that wasn't true. He'd tried his best with Teddy, but his best wasn't good enough. And that was worse. Knowing he simply wasn't the right man to guide Teddy into adulthood had him wishing that black hole would suck him up, put him out of his misery.

Radar crowded close and tried to lick his face. Gabe lifted his head and absently stroked the dog's ears.

The cold truth was that there was only one reason the thought of losing Addie hurt so much. He was in love with her. It wasn't the kissing or the fantastic sex; it was everything. Sitting on the steps and playing trivia fed something in his soul as nothing else had ever done.

He sighed and rubbed his hands up and down his face. *Great timing, Bishop.* He was in love—the forever and ever kind—with Addie.

And that was why he had to let her go. His heart was screaming at him to go and beg her to forgive him. But he had to be strong. His first instincts had been right. He wasn't the guy for them. They needed a guy who wasn't a screwup, a guy whose past wasn't fodder for town gossip.

For once in his life, he'd do the honorable thing and

truly mean it. He'd let them go, let them find some-body worthy of them. A woman like Addie needed her equal in life.

Gabe was still telling himself it was for the best two days later. He'd done his damnedest to avoid Addie and Teddy in the intervening time. He had to assume the court proceedings went well, because Teddy was still next door. If he weren't such a cow-ard, he'd go and ask or call her. But even though he loved them both, he wasn't what was best for them.

Radar jumped from the comfort of his dog bed and ran to the front door. Sure enough, a knock sounded.

Teddy stood on the stoop. His heart flipped over at the sight of the boy's healing black eye behind a new pair of glasses. Radar whined and nudged him as if to hurry him to open the door. The kid was probably here to ask if Radar could play. As much as he wanted to stay away from temptation, he was going to have a hard time telling the boy a flat-out no. After all, he'd come to care for Teddy like the boy was his own son.

Breathing deep, Gabe opened the door. "C'mon in."

Teddy shook his head but greeted and hugged Radar. "I just came to tell you something."

"Oh?"

Teddy took a deep breath and launched in. "You

told me that I shouldn't let being scared stop me from doing the right thing, but that's exactly what you're doing. With Addie, I mean."

"This is different." Was it? Was it really any different from what he'd told him? Was he protecting Addie or himself? "Where's your sister?"

"Addie's on the phone. She thinks I'm in my room, playing a game."

Teddy, with hands on hips and a mighty glower on his face, made quite the sight. "What happened at the hearing? Are you and Addie okay?"

"The judge says I can live with Addie forever if I want, but that's not what I came to say. Addie says you and her are taking a break, but my friend Ashley says that really means you're broken up. She said that's what her mom said when her dad left. But her dad never came back to live with them. Is it true that you're broken up?"

Gabe felt a pang of guilt. "It's complicated, Teddy, and—"

"Yeah, that's what Ashley said you'd say."

Gabe jerked his head back. Was his personal life a subject of discussion on the school playground? Before he could recover to form an appropriate response, Teddy started talking again.

"I wanted you to know that standing up to those kids when they picked on Sam was scary, but I did it, and now they leave Sam alone. I got a black eye, and it hurt, but it was worth it and I'd do it again." Teddy sniffed and wiped his nose on his sleeve. "Telling all those strangers why I wanted to live with Addie was scary, but I did it. Seems to me some of the best stuff is the scariest.

"Addie told me that she was scared of dogs because, she said, you said it was the right thing to do. So how come you can go around telling everyone else what to do and to not be scared, but then you hurt my sister because you're a coward?"

Well, this was a novel experience. He was used to military brass busting him, not a seven-year-old. One thing was the same, though. He'd have to swallow his feelings and not lash out. And besides, Teddy was right. "Is that what she told you? That I was a coward?"

"Nah. She said stuff to make you look good, but that's what Addie does. Maybe you fooled her, but you ain't foolin' me. You're scared and you don't want to be, so you broke up with my sister. But guess what—we don't need you."

Hearing those words felt like ice stabbing his heart. "Teddy, I'm sorry, but sometimes—"

"And you know what else? I think the way adults handle things is stupid."

The kid had him there. This wasn't the first time he'd bailed when the going got tough. He tried to tell himself this was different. That Addie was young and had her whole life ahead of her. *And what are you?* his inner voice asked. Sure, he was a few years older than her, but she'd gone through a lot in her young life and was probably more mature than him. She'd been willing to put her life, her dreams, on hold to take care of her little brother.

He believed Teddy when he said Addie hadn't bad-mouthed him. As Teddy said, that was what Addie did. The kid was right about something else too. He didn't deserve someone like Addie, but he was selfish enough to want her. What did that make him?

Radar looked from one to the other and began to whine. Teddy looked as if he might start crying at any minute, but he straightened up and faced Radar. "Gabe will have to explain to you why, if we won't be able to be friends anymore. It's up to him, but you'll always be the bestest dog in the world to me."

He hugged the dog and gave him a kiss on top of his head. Then he turned and left, going back to his side of the duplex and shutting the door quietly behind him. Leaving Gabe's heart broken into a million little pieces. So many pieces, he doubted he'd ever be able to even find them all if he tried.

Radar stood in the still-open doorway and cried. Talk about a pitiful noise. Finally, he gave Gabe a glower to match Teddy's, hung his head and slunk back to his bed. If Gabe didn't already feel like crap, this would do it for sure. He shut the door, wondering if he was shutting out the best part of his life.

Once Addie thought it over, she'd probably be

glad to be rid of him. He didn't exactly have a very good track record when it came to relationships. He couldn't even stick with the marines all the way to a full career and military retirement. He could have told her to ask Tracy. Gabe knew people in town tended to blame her for the divorce because they liked thinking of him as some sort of war hero. So of course, it couldn't have been his fault. When, in reality, it rested squarely on his shoulders. Tracy probably thought so.

He'd been reckless when he'd gotten Tracy pregnant. Maybe marrying her had been reckless too. He just hurt everyone he came in contact with—and he cared about Addie and Teddy too much to hurt them anymore.

Gabe spent a restless night, but by the next morning, he'd made a decision. He found Radar in his dog bed, his head on his front paws, looking like he carried the weight of the world.

Gabe jingled the leash, but the dog didn't budge. "So, you're still mad at me? How about if I told you I not only came to a decision, but I also have a plan?"

Radar made noises deep in his throat, a cross between a whine and a growl, but he crawled out of bed and trotted over.

"Let's hope when all is said and done, Addie is as forgiving as you."

Chapter Fifteen

Gabe shuffled his feet as Tracy held the door open and stared at him. She looked good. Older, more mature, of course. Her long brown hair that she'd always been so proud of was now chin length. But she was unmistakably still the same woman he'd married—and left—years earlier.

What had made him think this was such a good idea? He'd contacted old classmates until someone was able to give him her current address in a fashionable Boston suburb. He cussed and mentally dropped money into Teddy's swear jar. Except he didn't have the right to do that anymore.

"Gabe? Is it really you? How did you find me?"

"In the flesh," he said, expecting her to slam the door of the modest two-story home in his face. When she didn't but continued to stare at him, he cleared his throat. "Guess you never expected or wanted to see me again."

"Believe it or not, I've wanted to contact you over the years but always chickened out."

"Really?" He would have figured she'd been glad to see the last of him. He wasn't sure how to feel about her admission that she'd thought about him over the years.

"Yes, really." She touched his arm. "Come in. Please."

His first instinct was to tell her this was all a mistake and to run. As fast and as far as he could. But Teddy's accusing voice calling him a coward shouted in his head, and he grabbed the door his ex-wife was holding. "Thanks."

He followed her into an elegant living room. As he glanced around, he thought of Addie and Teddy's living room with its mismatched, flea-market furnishings, a room that was lived-in and charming. A room he wanted to share with the two of them—forever, he knew, if he could figure out a way to make that happen after the stupid stuff he'd said. But first he needed to close the book on the past. He recalled seeing one of those motivational posters that said something to the effect that you couldn't see the future if you were always looking back. Well, he was done looking back. Addie and Teddy *were* his future—if he could get over his own history.

Tracy pointed to an upholstered wingback chair. "Have a seat. Can I get you a coffee or anything?"

He shook his head. At the moment, he wasn't sure he could keep anything down. "No, thanks. I hope I'm not interrupting anything."

"No. My son won't be home from his playdate for at least an hour."

"You have a son?" Why should he be surprised? Of course she'd moved on, because that was what people did. And what he finally hoped to do too.

"Yes. Greg is five. He'll start kindergarten next fall."

"I'm happy for you." And he meant every word.

"What about you? Do you have any kids?"

"Not yet."

She smiled. "That sounds like you have plans."

"I'm hoping so." If Addie would have him and Teddy forgave him. He'd find a way. Marines got things done even when missions went sideways.

"Gabe, I want you to know I regret not reaching out to you before officially starting the divorce proceedings. I know we'd called it quits that last time you came home, but it still felt wrong somehow."

"To be honest, I was pissed when I got the papers, but I was also relieved," he admitted. "For that feeling alone, I think I deserve your scorn. I'm ashamed to even admit it."

"Sorry to disappoint you, Gabe, but I don't hold any animosity toward you. At first I did, but only because you were able to escape and I wasn't."

"Escape?" he questioned but had to admit the word was an apt description. His feelings of relief at getting away from the mess he had made of his life had mired him in guilt.

She shrugged. "We were kids in over our heads. I know that now."

"I was scared but thought I'd done the right thing by marrying you."

"You did the honorable thing, but I'm not convinced it was the right thing. We were too young. And once we lost our child, there was nothing left holding us together."

Tracy's words about honor echoed Addie's. God, how he missed her and Teddy. He could see by Tracy's expression, the tone of her voice, that she was happy. Probably settled in a relationship based on love and commitment. Oh, how he longed for that with Addie and Teddy. He wanted to be there through good times and bad, building a life in Loon Lake, raising Teddy and adding to their family when the time was right.

"Do you have someone special in your life? The way you said 'not yet' made it seem like there is someone."

He sighed. "I did, but, well, it's complicated."

"Do you love her?"

"I do." Huh, that was easy to admit. Why was he able to acknowledge that to his ex-wife and not to the one woman who actually mattered?

"Then I think you should be telling her, not me. I don't know what you did to make you say 'it's complicated,' but you should know, an apology goes a long way."

"This may take more than an apology."

"Want to talk about it? Maybe I can help?"

"You'd do that?" He was surprised. She really had forgiven him.

"Sure." She shrugged. "You're not the enemy, Gabe. You're not even a bad guy. Like I said, we were kids. I hope you haven't been shouldering guilt all this time."

"I was the one who was able to escape and leave you to deal. I'm not proud of that."

"Well, considering I was pushing you away, the fact you left didn't come as a surprise. Even if you'd stayed, I can't say that we would have been able to make the marriage work long-term."

"That may be true, but I still wanted to apologize to you." She might be letting him off the hook, but he needed to follow through on why he came. He wasn't letting himself off the hook. He needed to complete the mission, so he could go back to Addie and Teddy with a clean slate.

"Apologize?" She frowned and tilted her head. "For what?"

Did she truly not blame him? "For running when stuff got tough."

"Why would you think you owed me that? I initiated the divorce. If anyone should be saying they're sorry, it's me." She touched her open palm to her chest.

"But I abandoned you."

She shook her head. "And here all this time, I thought you'd joined the marines."

Okay, she had a point. Why was she so willing to forgive, though, when he couldn't do the same for himself? "But then I went overseas and left you to deal with everything here."

"It wasn't like my waitressing job was enough to support us." She shrugged. "And we had no medical insurance. You did what you had to."

"Then why the divorce?"

"We got married because I was pregnant. When I lost the baby, I didn't see any reason to stay together. I'm sorry. I…I shouldn't have handled it the way I did. I've carried the guilt of that."

"I know it may not have seemed like it at the time, but I did grieve the son we lost," he said softly. They'd barely had time to deal with losing their son when he'd shipped out.

He'd pushed away or stuffed down his grief, but even in Afghanistan, those feelings had sneaked up on him. He'd see local women with their children and be overcome, trying to deal with how raw and hollow he felt.

"Then put him to rest." She reached out and touched his knee. "Took me a while and a good therapist, but I've moved on and I'm happy. I'd like to think you were too."

"Is that your son? He's cute." He pointed to a picture on a side table. "All I can manage at the moment is a dog."

"Do you have a picture of your dog?"

He raised his eyebrows. "Really?"

"Really. I'm curious because there was a lot of emotion behind your statement." She laughed. "That's what three years of analysis can do."

"I'm sorry about your therapy. I—"

"Getting help was about me. Not you. And it was a good thing, so no need to apologize. Sounds like maybe you should consider it."

He grunted and pulled out his phone. Therapy? Would it help him get Addie back into his life? He'd do whatever it took to work through his issues—as evidenced by the fact he was with Tracy right now. He scrolled through his saved photos until he came to his favorite. He handed her the phone.

"Who is the boy?" She raised her head from the device to look at him before she handed it back.

"My neighbor's kid," he said quickly and glanced at the picture before slipping the cell back into his pocket.

"Oh? Sounds like more."

He shrugged and chuckled. "It's just that it was a case of love at first sight for the boy and the dog."

"You look kinda smitten too."

"Teddy's a good kid. Been through a lot in his young life. He lives with his sister because their mom is a drug addict."

"His sister? How old is she?"

"Twenty-two—no, make that twenty-three. Her birthday was last month." He couldn't help remembering that night after the opera. He laughed. "Teddy got it into his head that Addie wanted to go to the opera. Not sure where he got that notion, but I bought tickets and went to my first-ever opera."

"Gabriel Bishop at the opera?" She looked at him with amused wonder. "I would have paid good money to see that."

"I went. Turns out she isn't any more of an opera fan than I am." He grinned and shook his head. "We're still not sure what gave him that idea."

"Maybe he was playing a joke on you."

"I wondered that at first, but he was so proud of his suggestion, we knew he'd been serious. Neither one of us had the heart to tell him the truth."

"Sounds pretty serious to me."

He opened his mouth, but the denial died before it made it past his lips. Who was he kidding, except himself? The tightness that had dogged his chest since leaving Loon Lake finally began to ease. He inhaled deeply. "I love them."

"Do they know that?"

"Not yet."

She smiled at his simple statement and took his hand. "You know, I felt guilty for a long time too. Then I met Mitch and decided to forgive myself, to have a family and a future with someone I loved. Isn't it time for you to do the same?"

Maybe it was. All that time spent feeling guilty suddenly seemed like such a waste. Teddy called him a coward. Damn, but the label fit. He'd used his failed marriage as an excuse over the years, when it was really fear that had kept him from giving his heart again.

Teddy was 100 percent right. He *was* a coward… and would continue to be unless he told Addie and her brother how he really felt about them.

After he said goodbye to Tracy, he used the key fob to unlock the Jeep's door and opened it. He stood for a moment beside the vehicle, looking back at the house. It looked like a happy home and he was glad for Tracy.

He felt as if a weight had been lifted from his shoulders. One that he hadn't even realized he'd been carrying around all this time. Sure, he'd regretted the way he'd handled things, but he had done such a good job of pushing it into the background that his relief came as a surprise.

Getting in his Jeep, he started the engine.

"I have to do something to make this right."

He pulled away from the curb without a backward glance. He was through living in the past, through letting old mistakes—especially ones made when he was a teenager—ruin his future. He'd hurt both Addie and Teddy, and it wasn't going to be easy to win them back, but he wasn't going to give up. Failure wasn't an option.

Back in Loon Lake, he stopped at the Pic-N-Save and purchased a bouquet of flowers. He figured they couldn't hurt. If she wasn't in a forgiving mood, she could always throw them in his face.

Checking his watch to be sure he had time to beg forgiveness before Teddy came home, he knocked on her door. And he thought he'd been nervous standing on Tracy's doorstep. This was way worse. Tracy was his past. Addie was his future.

She opened it, and he could have sworn she looked glad to see him. At least she hadn't slammed the door in his face. And she hadn't even seen the flowers yet. Of course, the way he was squeezing those stems, he'd probably strangled the life out of them.

"Gabe."

"Before you say anything, I want to apologize for acting like such a jerk." He swallowed. "And to tell you I went to see Tracy, my ex."

"You did?" She motioned him in.

He nodded. So far, so good. "I did. I needed to face the past in order to move forward. I needed to put that to rest."

"How did it go?" She moved into the living room.

He followed her. "It was hard but easy too. Huh, I guess that doesn't make much sense."

She sat on the sofa and pointed to the spot beside her. "It makes perfect sense. You have a lot of history together."

He sat beside her but resisted the urge to touch. He needed to clear the air first. "We were able to talk about what happened. I guess you could say we were finally able to grieve together for the son we'd lost. She made me understand that feeling guilty was preventing me from moving forward."

He swallowed and shifted, edging toward her. "And I definitely want to move forward...with you and Teddy."

"I want that too. I guess I was dealing with my own guilt over what happened to Teddy and I thought I had to give up my future to atone. I think that's why I have such trouble trusting. But since the judge granted me permanent custody of Teddy, I've tried to relax a bit. Michelle didn't even show for the hearing, so I guess I fretted for nothing." She sniffed and touched his arm. "I want you to know I have absolute faith in you. Gabe, I would trust you with our future."

She pointed at the drooping flowers. "Were those for something?"

He loosened his death grip on the wilting bouquet. "They were for you, but I swear they looked better in the store."

She gave him a smile that quivered. "Maybe they'll perk up in water. Do you want me to—?"

"No! I mean, I need to say something more first. You can laugh or kick me to the curb, but I need to say it."

"Yes?"

Okay, this wasn't quite as easy as it had been when he'd rehearsed it in his head. He swallowed. "Addie Miller, I love you and…and I love Teddy as if he were my own. I would be honored to call him my son and to make it legal, if you agree."

Her face crumpled and she began to cry. *Oh no, not crying. Please.* What was it about women's tears that lowered men's testosterone levels? He tossed the flowers aside and he did the only thing he could— pulled her into his arms and held her tight. He rubbed his hand in circles over her back as she sobbed against his shoulder.

She lifted her tearstained face to his. "I don't know why I'm crying."

"It's okay. You can let it out. I think you've been holding in a lot of stuff for a long time. You won't have to carry your burdens alone ever again."

He continued to rub her back to comfort her. He

hated her tears, but if that was what she needed for healing, then he'd put up with it. But, by God, after today, he'd do his best to never give her a reason to cry again.

As her tears subsided, he brushed the hair off her face and wiped her cheeks with his thumbs. "Sorry I'm not the kind of guy who carries a handkerchief to assist ladies in distress."

She made a sound that was half laugh, half sob. "You're perfect the way you are."

"That's a good start, because you're not getting rid of me. I love you."

She caressed his face. "And I love you."

Several hours later, they sat on the front steps watching Teddy and Radar playing with a Frisbee. It had taken a little convincing to get Teddy to forgive him, but with Radar's help, he'd managed it. A sincere apology hadn't hurt, either.

His chest expanded as if trying to contain all the things he was feeling. Happy and proud that he'd figured out how to put his life back on track before it was too late. He'd made mistakes in the past and, no doubt, would again, but he'd never do anything to jeopardize his family's happiness. His family. He liked the sound of that.

He was still figuring out what he wanted to do, unsure if construction was for him in the long haul. It was good, honest work while Addie pursued her dream of a degree in library science. Thanks to his pa and the time they'd spent tinkering with those castoffs, Gabe had agreed to help Ogle open and run a small engine repair business next to his garage.

He watched Teddy toss the Frisbee for Radar and silently thanked his pa for everything he'd taught him, including how to be a good dad to Teddy.

Addie turned to him. "I have something to ask you…and you don't have to do it if you don't want to. No pressure."

He took her hand. "Do what?"

"I think you should be the one to accompany Teddy to the Cub Scout lock-in."

"Are you sure?" He squeezed her hand.

She nodded. "It's only fair. I know how hard you two worked on the Pinewood Derby race car. I hate to swoop in at the last minute and snatch all the glory when you guys win."

"You're that confident we're going to triumph?" He joked, but he knew how important this was. Teddy was her heart. She was granting him access to her heart, making him truly a part of their lives. And he wanted to seize the moment with all the joy he felt.

"I have confidence in you," she said and leaned over to kiss him.

He kissed her back, knowing her statement was about more than just the race car.

"Yuck, you guys." Teddy paused his game and shook his head. "Quit the mushy stuff."

Gabe pulled back and laughed. "Never."

Epilogue

Six months later

Gabe touched the box in his pocket as he paced and waited for Teddy. Head on his paws, Radar lay in his bed, his eyes following him as he crisscrossed the room.

Why was he so nervous? Although he and Addie maintained their own places, they'd been practically inseparable ever since their reconciliation. Many a morning he'd left her place before sunrise to return to his side of the duplex. They wanted to set a good example for Teddy—both of them. Although, he wasn't sure who was fooling who. The kid was as sharp as a tack. And Gabe couldn't be prouder of him if he'd been his own son. Which hopefully one day he would be. He and Addie had discussed adopting Teddy, so they'd officially be his parents.

Radar jumped up and ran to the door with Gabe on his heels.

"Hey, Gabe. I'm here like you told me this morning."

Gabe had asked Teddy to come straight to his place after school. He grinned at the boy.

"You are."

"Is anything wrong?"

"No, but I wanted to talk to you about something."

Teddy nodded solemnly, and he and Radar went to sit on the couch.

"You know your sister and I have been…have been…"

"Together?" Teddy supplied and grinned.

Gabe laughed. "Yeah. I'd like to make it, uh, permanent."

Teddy scrunched up his face. "Huh?"

"I'm going to ask your sister to marry me."

Teddy jumped up and whooped, causing Radar to dance around and bark.

Relief swept through him and Gabe laughed at the two of them. "Does this mean I have your permission?"

"Oh yeah! Does this mean Radar and I are brothers now?"

"I guess it does—if your sister says yes."

"She will." He nodded. "Does this mean I could… maybe…like call you Dad?"

Gabe tried to swallow past the sudden lump in his throat so he could respond. Teddy was looking up at him, no doubt waiting for an answer, and he couldn't get his voice to work, so he knelt and opened his arms.

Teddy threw himself at Gabe. "Dad."

"Son," Gabe managed to choke out. He couldn't believe how right that sounded, how it made him weak and strong at the same time. In that moment, as he hugged Teddy, he thanked his own pa for setting such a good example.

Radar pushed his nose between them, wanting in on the action. They both laughed and pulled apart enough to include the dog.

"How about we make the dad stuff official too?" Gabe suggested.

"What does *official* mean?"

"It means I would be your dad forever."

"What about Addie?"

"We'd both adopt you and she'd be your mom."

"Hear that, Radar? I have a real mom and dad now and we're all gonna live together forever and ever."

The doorbell rang and Radar rushed over, barking.

"Radar, stop," Gabe ordered, and the dog immediately stopped barking and sat down in front of the door.

"Hey, come on in," Gabe greeted Des Gallagher.

"Sorry if I'm late." Des came in but didn't shut the door. "Sam's in the car."

"No. Perfect timing."

"What are you doing here, Mr. Des? Why is Sam in the car?"

"I've come to invite you to play miniature golf with Sam and me. Afterward, we're going for pizza. How's that sound?"

"Right now?"

"Sure. That's why I'm here to pick you up." Des turned to Gabe. "I thought you were going to speak to him."

"I did… I am." Gabe shrugged. "We didn't get to that part yet."

"What part?" Teddy asked.

"The part where you come with Sam and me," Des told him.

"But—but it's happening now. I'll miss it," Teddy said.

"What's happening now?" Addie asked from the doorway. "What's going on?"

Gabe started laughing. When was the last time any of his plans had gone off without a hitch? He sighed and got down on one knee. "This is what's happening now."

Des leaned down and whispered something in Teddy's ear.

"Yuck. Mushy stuff. I'm going with Mr. Des and Sam."

Addie watched Teddy and Des leave, then turned back to Gabe, who was still down on one knee.

"Addie Miller, will you marry me?" He took the box out of his pocket and opened it.

She dropped to her knees in front of him and threw her arms around him. "Yes, I'll marry you."

He slipped the simple but elegant diamond solitaire on her finger. She threw her arms around him again, and he hugged her tight and kissed her as pure joy flooded his body.

Radar sat on the floor next to them and woofed. They both laughed. Addie reached out to pet the dog and whispered, "Thank you, Radar."

* * * * *

Don't miss the previous volumes in
Carrie Nichols's Small-Town Sweethearts series:

The Scrooge of Loon Lake
His Unexpected Twins
The Sergeant's Unexpected Family
The Marine's Secret Daughter

Available now from Harlequin Special Edition!

*Skylar Davis is grateful to have her late husband's dog.
But the struggling widow can barely keep her three
daughters fed, much less a hungry canine. Kyle Mitchell
was her husband's best friend and he can't stop himself
from rescuing them. But will his exposed secrets ruin
any chance they have at building a family?*

Read on for a sneak peek at
Their Rancher Protector,
*the latest book in the Texas Cowboys & K-9s miniseries
by* USA TODAY *bestselling author Sasha Summers!*

"Even the strongest people need a break now and then. It's
not a sign of being weak—it's part of being human," he
murmured against her temple. "As far as I'm concerned,
you're a badass."

She shook her head but didn't say anything.

"Look at your girls," he insisted. "You put those smiles
on their faces. You found a way to keep them entertained
and positive and with enough imagination to turn that
leaning wooden shack into a playhouse—"

"Hey," she interrupted, peering up at him with red-
rimmed eyes.

"I was teasing." He smiled. "You're missing the point
here."

"Oh?" She didn't seem fazed by the fact that she was still holding on to him—or that there was barely any space between them.

But he was. And it had him reeling. The moment her gaze met his, the tightness and pressure in his chest gave way. And having Skylar in his arms, soft and warm and all woman, was something he hadn't prepared himself for.

Focus. Not on the unnerving reaction Skylar was causing, but on being here for Skylar and the girls. *Focus on honoring Chad's last request.* Chad—who'd expected him to take care of the family he'd left behind, not get blindsided and want more than he should. How could he not? Skylar was a strong, beautiful woman who had his heart thumping in a way he didn't recognize.

"Thank you, again." Her gaze swept over his face before she rose on tiptoe and kissed his cheek. "You're a good man, Kyle Mitchell."

Don't miss
Their Rancher Protector *by Sasha Summers,*
available August 2021 wherever
Harlequin Special Edition books and ebooks are sold.

Harlequin.com

HSEEXP0721

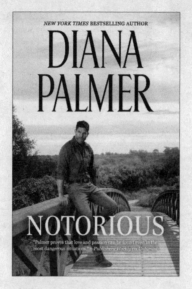

Love Harlequin romance?

DISCOVER.

Be the first to find out about promotions, news and exclusive content!

Facebook.com/HarlequinBooks

Twitter.com/HarlequinBooks

Instagram.com/HarlequinBooks

Pinterest.com/HarlequinBooks

ReaderService.com

EXPLORE.

Sign up for the Harlequin e-newsletter and download a free book from any series at **TryHarlequin.com**

CONNECT.

Join our Harlequin community to share your thoughts and connect with other romance readers!
Facebook.com/groups/HarlequinConnection

HSOCIAL2020